Over the Cliff

Joe took a rope and tied it tightly around his waist.
Frank did the same. Then both boys tied the other
ends of the ropes securely around a big tree near the
edge of the cliff.

Soon the brothers were edging down the cliff face,
grabbing handholds wherever they could find them.
For the most part, there were plenty of places to get a
good footing. Finally, though, they came to a place
where they were hanging over the edge of a precipice.
"Boy, these ropes better hold," Frank said. "Once we
get past here, it's clear sailing to the bottom."

Just as he said it, though, he felt his rope give way a
little.

"Hey!" he cried, his heart leaping to his throat.
"What the—?"

At that moment, there was a twanging sound from
above them, and Frank felt his rope give way altogether.

"Joe!" he cried. "I'm falling!"

The Hardy Boys Mystery Stories

Available from MINSTREL Books

125

The HARDY BOYS®

MYSTERY ON
MAKATUNK ISLAND

FRANKLIN W. DIXON

A MINSTREL® BOOK

PUBLISHED BY POCKET BOOKS

New York   London   Toronto   Sydney   Tokyo   Singapore

A MINSTREL PAPERBACK *ORIGINAL*

A Minstrel Book published by
POCKET BOOKS, a division of Simon & Schuster Inc.
1230 Avenue of the Americas, New York, NY 10020

ISBN: 0-671-79315-2

First Minstrel Books printing April 1994

10 9 8 7 6 5 4 3 2 1

Printed in the U.S.A.

Contents

MYSTERY ON
MAKATUNK ISLAND

1 Island of Crime

"Watch out, Frank!" Joe Hardy shouted to his older brother. But it was too late. A wave hit the bow of the *Maine Maiden,* sending a wall of spray over the rail of the small ferry directly onto Frank's head. Joe had managed to duck against the cabin wall just in time to avoid getting drenched himself.

"Whew!" Frank shouted, vigorously shaking water from his thick dark hair as he steadied himself at the rail. "The ocean's a little choppy this morning."

"That's an understatement," Joe called, pushing against the wall for better balance. "All the other passengers are inside the cabin, in case you didn't notice. Not many people like saltwater showers."

"This is my idea of fun, Joe," Frank said, whisking water off his red vinyl poncho. "Surrounded by

1

fog, the salt spray in our faces, cutting through the waves. It's great!" He looked around. "Where's Chet? He shouldn't be missing this."

"He's lying down in the cabin," Joe said. "Between the rough sea and the extra sausage he had this morning at breakfast, he isn't feeling too well."

"Let's go see how he's doing," Frank said, walking to the double doors of the cabin and pushing them open.

The blue and gray cabin looked to Frank as if it were designed to seat about fifty passengers. But almost all the wooden benches were empty. Only about a dozen people were traveling to Makatunk Island on this foggy day.

Chet Morton, the Hardys' best friend, was stretched out across a bench. His eyes were closed, and his skin looked faintly green. "How's it going, Chet?" Frank asked, walking over to him.

"Okay, I guess." Chet groaned. "How long till we get there?"

"It'll be about half an hour," Joe said. "Makatunk Island is a good fifteen miles off the Maine coast."

"I'll never make it," Chet said.

"Next time you go sailing, don't chow down on a big meal first," Joe said. Brushing his blond hair off his forehead, he sat across from Chet, looking sympathetically at his husky friend.

"Hang in there, Chet," Frank said encouragingly. "Soon you'll be off this boat and at your aunt Emma's house, ready for a week of fun and relaxation. Hiking on woodland trails, dining on fresh lobster—"

"Please," Chet broke in. "Don't mention food."

"It was nice of your aunt to offer us the place for the week, since the house is vacant," Joe said. "How come she's not coming out, though?"

"She hardly ever comes to Makatunk anymore. She's too busy with her job in the city," Chet said. "The house has been a good source of extra income for her, though. Until this year, anyway."

"I can't figure out why she's having trouble finding tenants," Frank said. "Makatunk Island is supposed to be the most beautiful spot on the Maine coast. It ought to be packed during the summer."

"Usually it is," Chet said. "But this year two tenants canceled on her and—oohhhh!" Another wave rocked the boat, and Chet covered his face with his hands.

Frank looked around the cabin to see if anyone else looked as if they were feeling seasick. There was a family with four children who were sprawled across the benches, playing tic-tac-toe. The mother was reading a book, and the father was looking out the cabin window, relaxing. A few rows up from them sat a gray-haired couple, eating oranges. The rocking boat didn't seem to bother any of them in the least. In the back of the cabin were a young Asian man and woman, holding hands and gazing into each other's eyes. Frank wondered if they were on their honeymoon.

The only other passengers were two men sitting by the door. In their suits and ties, they looked as if they had just stepped from a corporate suite onto the ferry. The dark-haired man wore glasses and was working on a laptop computer. The blond one sat fidgeting, tapping his fingers and staring down at their luggage.

"Those guys look like they've never been outdoors in their lives," Frank whispered to Joe. "I wonder what made them want to come to Makatunk."

Joe shrugged and looked at the cabin door as it swung open. In came an older man with a gray beard and a dark blue sea captain's hat. "Rough passage this morning. Everyone okay?" he called out, looking around.

"When will we get there?" Chet groaned. He pulled himself up to a sitting position. "I feel like I've been on this boat forever."

"Ayeh." The bearded man nodded. "There's always one landlubber." He laughed loudly and gave Chet a hard pat on the back. Chet grimaced and placed his hands firmly down on the bench on either side of him to steady himself. "Thank your stars you came in summer, lad. You wouldn't want to be on the *Maine Maiden* for a winter voyage!"

The man turned to the rest of the passengers. "Folks, I'm your captain," he explained. "Name's William Smith, but you can call me Gabby. Everyone else does."

"Uh, Gabby?" the mother of the children asked.

4

"I hope this isn't a silly question, but if you're out here, who's steering the boat?"

Gabby laughed again, showing a few missing teeth. "Oh, don't you worry any, ma'am," he assured her. "She's on automatic pilot. We're in open ocean now. When it's time, I'll go back to the bridge and guide her in. Got room for one in there, if any of you'd like to come up front with me," he added.

"Mommy, look!" one of the children cried, pointing out the window. "The fog is going away!"

Frank peered out the cabin window and smiled. Streaks of sunlight were piercing through the clouds, and a big chunk of sky had appeared.

"If anybody wants to get a look at Makatunk, just head up to the bow," Gabby suggested. "It's a pretty sight."

All four children ran for the cabin door at once. "Stay away from the railing, kids!" their father shouted as he followed after them.

Joe got up, too. "I think I'll have a look," he said. "Frank? Want to come?"

"No thanks," Frank said. "I'd like to check out the bridge and see how the *Maine Maiden* is steered, if that's okay with you," he said, turning to Gabby.

"Fine by me," Gabby answered.

"Thanks." Frank followed the captain up the short flight of metal steps that led from the cabin to the bridge. It was a closet-size space enclosed by thick glass windows. From there, across the open sea, Frank saw Makatunk Island rising from the water like a huge humpbacked whale.

"It feels a lot farther from the mainland than I thought it would. Almost like another world," Frank said. He looked over at the captain, who held the large wooden wheel in his weathered hands.

"Ayeh, another world." Gabby nodded, and smiled. "A world that can only be reached by boat."

"How many people live on the island?" Frank asked.

"Oh, about a hundred-fifty, year-round," Gabby replied. "But usually, during the summer, I bring over as many as two hundred visitors a day." He sighed sadly. "Not this year, though."

"Why not?" Frank asked. "What's going on?"

Gabby looked him over carefully. "You Emma Morton's nephew?" he asked.

"No, that's my friend Chet," Frank told him. "The one who isn't feeling well."

"Ah, the landlubber!" Gabby said with a laugh. "I see."

"I'm Frank Hardy. The blond-haired guy is my brother, Joe. We're staying at Emma's for the week."

"Haven't seen Emma up here in quite a while," Gabby said. "She mostly rents her place out nowadays. So do a lot of people who own houses on the island. That's the problem, if you ask me."

"I don't understand," Frank said.

"See, back when I was a kid, Makatunk was just a

6

quiet fishing island," Gabby explained. "If you didn't mind the simple life and could do without things most people take for granted, like electricity, or cars, even a central telephone service, then Makatunk was a peaceful and cheap place to live. But pretty soon word of its beauty and simple ways spread. First the artists came, drawn by the beauty of the place, and a lot of them settled in and built houses. Makatunk became a real artist colony. Some of our artists got to be pretty famous, too. Maybe a little too famous. Ever hear of Kent Halliwell?"

"Sure," Frank said. "Who hasn't?"

"Well, she's got a place on Makatunk, out by the shipwreck. Big gray and white house. Anyway, more and more people wanted to have a look at the island, and the more they saw, the more they liked. Pretty soon the place was flooded with tourists. Some were day-trippers come to get a gander at Ms. Halliwell and the celebrity friends she brings over with her. Others came and rented for the season. But the way I see it, no temporary resident is going to care about the island the way a year-rounder does. It's just not in human nature. I see day-trippers down at the wharf, tossing candy wrappers on the ground like it's their personal wastebasket."

"That's awful," Frank said. He knew how thoughtless campers could quickly spoil a site.

"And the tourists brought up the prices, too! It's got so people like me can hardly afford to live here anymore." Gabby shook his head sadly. "We've even got crime now, like every other place."

7

"Crime?" Frank's ears perked up. Even though he was only eighteen and Joe was seventeen, the brothers were experienced detectives, and neither one of them could resist investigating a crime wherever they found it.

"Ayeh. It started this past winter with graffiti and knocked-over garbage cans. We thought it was just the island kids making mischief. But there aren't many kids on Makatunk. They all go to the same one-room school, and they're a pretty good crop. Oh, there was a boy who was fairly troublesome, but that was some years ago. Anyhow, we soon came to realize it wasn't the kids causing the problems." Gabby paused and then nodded to Frank. "Cover your ears, lad."

Not understanding, Frank covered his ears as Gabby pushed a button. A loud horn blasted, warning the islanders of the boat's approach.

Frank could see the island clearly now. At one end of the rocky shore was a rusty old shipwreck, half-submerged in the water near the shoreline. Near it was the gray and white house that Gabby had described as belonging to Kent Halliwell, the artist. Toward the middle of the island was a wharf where people were gathering to meet the ferry. Most of the island's buildings seemed to be centered around the wharf and the hill behind it. Above the town were dark green highlands, in what appeared to be a completely natural state. It was difficult for Frank to imagine a more unlikely setting for a rash of crimes.

Frank turned from the picturesque view and back to the captain.

"You were saying that you didn't think kids were making the trouble. What do you mean?" Frank asked.

Gabby frowned. "Oh, the trouble got too serious for kids to be doing it," he explained. "We had broken windows, more than twenty. And, what's worse, someone started cutting lobster buoys loose. People around here make their living lobstering, you know."

"I know," Frank said, looking out. He could see dozens of round buoys bobbing in the sunlit sea.

"Every one of those little buoys represents a family's living," Gabby said, pointing to one nearby. "Once the buoy is cut, a man can never find his trap again. He's got to go out and buy a new one and start all over."

"That is serious," Frank said.

"It got so bad that the *Bar Harbor Times* ran a feature about the so-called crime wave on Makatunk." Gabby shook his head in disgust. "Well, that chased the tourists away pretty quick! I may not always love them, you know, but we depend on our visitors. If things don't turn around soon, I don't know what the end of it will be."

Frank looked at Gabby's worried face and then out at the beautiful island they were approaching. If there was trouble, he thought, maybe he and Joe could help. They were going to be here for a week. That ought to be enough time to investigate.

"I'd better go below," Frank said. "Thanks, Gabby. It was nice talking to you."

"My pleasure," Gabby said, smiling broadly. "I love to talk—that's why they call me Gabby!" Frank laughed and headed down the stairs. "See you on the trip back, if not before," Gabby called after him.

No one was in the cabin now, except for Chet, who was lying down and looking greener than ever. Everyone else had gone out on deck since the boat had entered the quiet waters of the harbor.

"You okay, buddy?" Frank asked Chet.

"Yeah, I feel great." Chet smiled weakly. He didn't bother to open his eyes.

"We're about to dock," Frank said. "Do you think you can stand up?"

"I don't know."

"Let's try. I think the fresh air will make you feel better." Frank helped Chet to his feet and led him out on deck. Joe was standing at the rail gazing out at the island. He turned as Frank and Chet approached.

"You never looked better, Chet," Joe joked.

"Ha, ha," Chet said flatly. "Very funny." He took a deep breath of the fresh island air and leaned weakly against the railing.

The boat had slowed down and was inching toward the crowded dock. It looked to Joe as if everyone on the island must have come to watch the ship arrive. "This must be the big event of the day in a quiet place like this," he remarked.

Frank quickly told Joe and Chet what Gabby had said. "Hmm," Joe murmured. "Maybe things aren't as peaceful as they look."

When the boat stopped, the boys got off. They walked into the small crowd and waited for their luggage to come ashore. Though Joe and Frank had packed lightly for the week, Chet had brought up a large easel that his aunt had asked him to transport. She hoped that by providing it, she might attract an artist looking for a rental.

Frank, Joe, and Chet watched as a few men loaded up their trucks with cargo that had been on the boat. There were boxes of food, household goods, fishing gear, and other things the store owners and islanders needed.

"I thought cars weren't allowed on the island," Joe said, nodding toward a nearby truck.

"Cars, not trucks," Chet corrected him. "You should be glad, Joe. If there were no trucks we'd have to carry everything up the hill to the house!"

The Hardys and Chet watched as a muscular man in his early twenties hoisted their luggage off the ship and onto his truck. He had sun-streaked brown hair and a thick mustache, and he wore a green and black checkered shirt.

"Those are our bags," Frank told the man, walking up to him. "They're going up to the Morton house." He extended his hand. "I'm Frank Hardy."

The man stared at Frank's hand, but he didn't shake it. "Dollar a bag," he said flatly. "Two for anything bulky."

11

Frank paid him, then walked back to Joe and Chet. "Not exactly a warm welcome from the locals," he said.

Suddenly there was a commotion on the other side of the dock. Two men were throwing punches at each other as a crowd gathered. "Why did you do it, Farley? Why'd you cut my buoys?" shouted one, a wiry man with blond hair in a red T-shirt.

"I never touched them, Edgar!" shouted the other, a tall bald man in worn overalls. "You're just trying to throw suspicion on me because you stole my new traps!"

"Are you calling me a thief, Farley?" Edgar yelled. "Are you?" In a fit of rage, Edgar picked up a crowbar that was lying on the ground and raised it high over his head. "Because if you are, I swear I'll kill you right here and now!"

2 Sinking Fast!

In an instant Frank and Joe sprang into action. Frank, who was six feet one, delivered a flying kick to the wrist of the man holding the crowbar, sending it hurtling off the dock and into the water. Joe, six feet tall and muscular, restrained the man called Farley, while Frank grabbed Edgar, the would-be assailant. "Let me at him!" Edgar cried, struggling as Frank held his hands tightly behind his back.

"What's going on here?" a silver-haired man called out as he came through the crowd at the edge of the dock. He wore a freshly pressed dark blue work shirt and gray pants. A small notepad and pen peeked out from his shirt pocket. The man shook his head sadly. "You fellas at it again?"

"Morning, sheriff," Farley mumbled. He quieted down, and Joe let him go. Edgar, too, relaxed enough to be released.

Edgar pointed an accusing finger at the bald man. "He did it again, Sherm," Edgar insisted. "He cut my buoys!"

"And who stole the lobster traps out of my shack? Tell me that, Edgar!" Farley countered.

"Calm down, both of you. Don't go taking the law into your own hands. It's not necessary." The sheriff calmly took a package of gum from his pocket and offered it to each man in turn. They both declined. "Neither of you has got a scrap of proof that the other did anything wrong. And, frankly, I'd doubt if either of you is the guilty party. But I'll tell you what. When I do find out who is cutting the buoys around here, I'm going to nail him, but good!"

"I suppose you're right," Edgar admitted. "I don't have real proof. Sorry I lost my temper, Farley."

"Well, all right," the bald man said. "Just understand, I didn't cut your buoys." He turned to the sheriff. "You're all right, Sherm. I'm glad I voted for you for sheriff."

"Me, too," Edgar agreed. "It's good to have a fellow fisherman in charge of things. But you'd better find the bad apple who's behind all this mess, fast. Any more of this, and I'm selling my house and moving to Florida."

"I'd like to see that," Farley said. "First hot day

and you'd be running back to Maine, screaming all the way!"

"You've got to stop the trouble, Sherm," Edgar pleaded. He picked up some gear and turned to leave.

"I promise you I'll do my best." The sheriff turned to the Hardys as the rest of the crowd broke up. "Thanks, boys," he said. "You were a big help. Name's Sherm Davis. As you probably heard, I'm the sheriff around here."

The Hardys introduced themselves and Chet, who had met the sheriff when he was a boy, said hello. "How's your aunt Emma?" Sherm asked. He smiled for the first time since they'd seen him. "Haven't seen her up here in a dog's age."

"Fine," Chet said wanly, and wiped his forehead.

"You look like the sea got to you, young fella," Sherm said with a chuckle.

"Mr. Davis," Frank broke in. "We've heard about what's been happening lately. Joe and I are detectives. If there's trouble here on the island, maybe we can help."

Sherm gave them a long, searching look. Frank wasn't sure what the man was thinking. Then Sherm said, "I don't know that you ought to go messing around, getting involved, boys. But if you want to come out with me this afternoon on my fishing boat, we can talk things over, I suppose."

Frank and Joe looked at each other excitedly. "You're on!" Joe said. "What time?"

"Meet me here at two," Sherm suggested.

"Not me," Chet said. "I think I'll just hang around up at the house."

"Are you sure, Chet?" Frank asked.

"Believe me," Chet said. "I've been on enough boats for one day."

With that, the boys took off toward Emma's house, which Chet told them was about a half mile away. They passed through the main part of town on their way. There was a coffee shop, an art gallery, several fishermen's shacks, and a general store—all old wooden buildings. Nothing on Makatunk looked modern in any way. They also passed a large old hotel whose sign read Makatunk Inn.

"Most of the buildings are close to town," Chet said. "The rest of the island is untouched. It's got trails, woods, even cliffs."

"Maybe we can camp out tomorrow night," Joe suggested.

"No," Chet said. "There's no camping allowed. The islanders can't take any chances with fire."

"Well, we can hike then," Joe said with a shrug as they continued up the dirt road away from town and up the hill.

Frank took in a deep whiff of the invigorating sea air. "This place is incredible!"

"I've seen a lot of For Sale signs, though," Joe observed, as they passed a small blue clapboard house with a real estate notice in the front yard.

"Aunt Emma said that if the rental market

16

doesn't pick up, she may try to sell, too," Chet said. "I hope she doesn't. I love this place."

They soon came to a crossroads, with a painted wooden sign that read Hawk's Hill Road. It led up an even steeper hill to their left. "My aunt's house is at the end of this road."

The houses along Hawk's Hill Road were fancier than those down below. Many were painted in unusual colors and had hand-painted shingles hanging out front. "Merry Haverstraw, Watercolors and Woodcuts. By Appointment Only," Joe read, passing a sign in front of a lavender house with pale yellow trim.

"Oil Portraits by Carl Colao," Chet read from another sign in front of a mint green house down the road. "Open to the Public two to five P.M. Except Mondays."

"I see what they mean about Makatunk being an artist colony," Joe said, smiling.

By the time they reached Emma's house at the top of the hill, Chet was out of breath. Even Frank and Joe, who were very athletic, were huffing and puffing a little.

"Boy, these hills are steep!" Joe said, catching his breath.

"Hello, there. Is that you, Chet?" called a short, thin woman of about sixty who was hanging up laundry in the yard next to Emma's house.

"Yes, Mrs. Johnson, hi!" Chet answered, meeting her at the picket fence between the houses.

"Why, I haven't seen you in two or three years,

Chet," Mrs. Johnson said. "You've filled out a little, but you look good."

Chet introduced Frank and Joe, then pointed to the sign on her lawn. "I'm surprised you want to sell your house. I know how much you love it here."

"Well, Chet," the neighbor said, "Makatunk isn't what it used to be."

"A lot of people are saying that same thing," Chet told her.

"We haven't had much interest from buyers, though," she said with a regretful smile. "Mr. Johnson says maybe we should stop trying and just stay put."

"Well, good luck, however it turns out," Chet said.

Frank, Joe, and Chet walked up to Emma's front steps just as the young man from the wharf pulled up and began unloading their bags. "Hi, I'm Joe," Joe said, grabbing a bag from the large man. "What's your name?"

"Dexter," the man mumbled. He dropped the last of the luggage onto the wrap-around porch. "Dollar a bag, and two for that thing," he said, pointing to the easel.

"But I paid at the wharf!" Frank protested.

"Pay at the bottom, and pay at the top," Dexter said evenly, holding out his palm.

Frank stood open-mouthed. The guy certainly had a lot of nerve! Rolling his eyes, Frank reached into his pocket and paid Dexter the extra money.

The young man pocketed the bills and roared away in his beat-up truck.

"Why'd you pay him?" Joe asked, clearly peeved.

"I don't know," Frank said. "I figured it wouldn't be good to make an enemy so soon. It's a small island."

"Well, let's get unpacked," Joe grumbled. He grabbed a bag and took it inside. "It's almost lunchtime."

"Ugh," Chet said. "Don't mention food."

"Really, Chet?" Joe said, a mischievous look in his eyes. "Not even a nice, juicy sausage sandwich?"

Emma's house was an old-fashioned white Victorian with pink shutters. It had a small parlor, a large kitchen, and two upstairs bedrooms. The front of the house had a breathtaking view of the ocean below, and the back faced a meadow full of blooming yellow wildflowers.

Chet took them upstairs. He was going to use his aunt's bedroom, and he pointed the Hardys toward the guest bedroom.

"This house is great," Joe said as he set his bag down.

"It looks really comfortable, too," Frank said, looking around. Emma's furniture was sturdy and old-fashioned. The twin beds were piled high with pillows and comforters. There were rag rugs scattered about, and an overstuffed chair and footstool sat near the window.

19

Joe and Frank quickly unpacked, then joined Chet in his room. "Anyone up for lunch, besides Chet, that is?" Joe asked.

"Very funny," Chet said, throwing himself down on Emma's four-poster bed. "I already told you I'm not going anywhere today. The way I feel, I might not leave the house all week."

"You and I will go then, Joe," Frank suggested. "Feel better, Chet. We'll be back in a while."

Joe and Frank headed downstairs and outside. They walked down the hill toward town. In the general store they bought a map of the island. Then they went to the coffee shop for a quick lunch.

As they ate their sandwiches, Joe unfolded the map. It was a photocopy of a hand-drawn map created by one of the island artists. "Every building on the island is marked on this map," Joe said, pointing to a tiny square. "Here's Emma's place. There's Hawk's Hill Road."

"Let's see," Frank said. He peered at the map. "Here's where we are now, at the coffee shop. There's the dock, and there's the shipwreck we saw from the boat. It says here it's the remains of a cargo ship that went down in 1852. And what's this? An ice house, built in 1817."

Joe turned the map sideways to get a better look at one particular section. "Wow!" he exclaimed. "Look how much of the island is empty."

"Not empty, Joe," Frank corrected him. "It's just not built up. What does it say by that asterisk?"

" 'This area of Makatunk Island is owned by a

20

group of islanders committed to the preservation of its natural state.' That's fantastic.''

"Yeah," Frank agreed. Then he remembered the fight on the dock that morning. "Too bad somebody's trying to mess things up around here.''

"Well, maybe there's something we can do about that," Joe said decisively. "It's almost two," he said, checking his watch and folding the map back up. "Let's see what we can find out from the sheriff.''

The brothers went outside and headed toward the dock. Even here, in the tiny town, Makatunk Island had a natural feel. The main road was just a wide dirt path. Since no cars were allowed on the island, the only traffic was a few people walking around, enjoying the day. Frank noticed the Asian couple, still holding hands as they stood in front of the general store. "Hi," the man said as Joe and Frank passed by.

"Hi," Joe responded. The white-haired couple who had been eating oranges on the boat stepped out of the general store. The man was holding out an island map in front of him.

"Hello, boys," the woman said with a smile.

In front of the art gallery, which looked like a converted carriage house, a red-haired woman was sweeping her slate doorstep. She nodded to the Hardys as well. "Good afternoon," she said, greeting them with a faintly European accent that Frank couldn't quite identify.

"Everyone's so friendly," Joe said.

"I guess it's hard not to be in a place like this.''

21

Frank noticed the two men who'd been in business suits coming out of a store that sold fishing gear. "Hi," he said.

The men looked startled for a second before they awkwardly returned the greeting. "I guess they're not used to people being friendly," Joe said with a grin.

Rounding the bend to the wharf, the Hardys came face-to-face with a group of about ten people, most holding open books in their hands. A quick glance told Frank they were plant identification books.

"You there, watch your step!" one of them, a tall, dark-haired woman called to Joe. "Those are indigenous plants underfoot!"

Joe looked down. All he saw was the rocky road and a tuft of weeds.

"Here," the woman said impatiently, bending down and pointing to a small patch of green. "This is plantain. It was a very important plant in Shakespeare's time. Please be careful not to trample it!"

"Nora, look—pigweed!" one of the group called from across the road. Giving Joe a final stern look, the dark-haired woman hurried off, taking care to avoid stepping on any greenery.

Joe turned to Frank in astonishment. "What was that all about?"

"Beats me," Frank said with a shrug.

Minutes later, the boys reached the wharf, where they found the sheriff filling the gas tank of his red and white fishing boat, the *Northern Lights,* from a pump at the side of the dock. The *Northern Lights* was a small vessel with tangled nets littering the stern. "Ahoy," Sherm hailed the Hardys. "Ready to catch yourselves some codfish?"

"Ready as we'll ever be," Frank said, grinning.

"Climb aboard, then," Sherm said. He held out a hand and helped Frank, then Joe onto the deck. Next to a pile of poles, Frank saw two large catch boxes, half filled with fresh water.

"Here goes nothing," Sherm said. After starting up the small boat, he expertly guided it through the harbor and out to the open sea. The noise of the engine was too loud for conversation until Sherm navigated around one end of the island and came to a place about a mile out from a rocky cove. There, he cut the engine and dropped anchor.

"This is where they've been biting all week," he said. "Grab a pole. I'll show you how to do it."

Twenty minutes later, the first few cod were thrashing around in the catch box on deck. "Sherm," Frank said, "on the way to the dock, we passed some people reading books and talking about weeds."

"Oh, yes, must have been Nora Stricter's Acorn Society," the sheriff said. "They come every summer, and stay over at the inn."

"What's the Acorn Society?" Joe asked.

"Oh, you'd best ask them about it. I wouldn't want to describe them wrong," Sherm said with a laugh. "They think everybody is out to harm the planet. I told Nora, 'Mighty nuts from tiny acorns grow.' Well, she didn't appreciate my little joke one bit."

"She chewed me out for trampling a weed," Joe said.

"That's Nora," Sherm said, shaking his head. "I wouldn't mind her half so much if she weren't always trying to convert people to her cause. For instance, they don't eat fish, which is fine and good, I suppose. But this is a fishing island! Sometimes I think she'd like to get every last fisherman off Makatunk, and have the place all to herself."

"That's very interesting," Frank said thoughtfully. "Who do you think is behind all the crimes that have been happening on the island?"

Sherm pulled out a pack of chewing gum. After offering some to Joe and Frank, Sherm slowly unwrapped a piece and popped it in his mouth. "That's a tough one. I can't think of anyone who would want to hurt the island or the people here."

"You just said Nora Stricter wanted to get rid of the fishermen," Frank pointed out.

"Hmmm, I did, didn't I?" Sherm said. "Well, maybe it's her, then. I'll have to look into it." He stood up and stretched. "You boys want a soda? I've got some below."

"Sure thing!" Joe said. "The salt air makes me thirsty."

"One for you, Frank?" Sherm asked.

"Thanks," Frank said.

"I've got popcorn, too, if you'll come and help

carry it up," Sherm said. Frank followed him into the cabin, where Sherm opened the hatch to the engine and storage compartment.

"What the——?" Sherm cried as he opened the hatch. "I'll be. We're taking on water!"

Frank looked down, and what he saw chilled him to the bone. A four-inch-deep pool of water lay on the bottom of the engine compartment, and more was pouring in through a three-inch hole in the boat, right next to the engine.

Sherm quickly ripped off his shirt and stuffed it into the hole. "I don't think this'll do much good," he said, his voice urgent. "Between a wet engine and a floor full of water, we're apt to sink like a stone!"

3 The Missing Traps

"What can I use to bail?" Frank shouted.

"There," Sherm answered, pointing to two buckets that were hanging from the cabin wall behind Frank. Frank grabbed one, and handed the other to Sherm. But Sherm waved it off. "I've got to go try to rev up the engine," he said, dashing past Frank to the controls.

"Joe!" Frank yelled up the steps. "Come quick!"

"What's up?" Joe asked, coming down the stairs. Frank didn't need to answer. The look on Joe's face showed that he understood at once. He grabbed the full bucket from Frank and ran back up to toss the water overboard. Then he came back down for another. It was a clumsy process, and the water was coming in much faster than they could bail it out.

"If the engine is wet, we're sunk!" Sherm called.

But, luckily, the motor sputtered to life. Sherm swung the boat around and headed for the port. Frank and Joe bailed as fast as they could, but they couldn't keep up with the incoming water.

"Grab some life jackets, boys. They're in here," Sherm said, reaching over to a cabinet and opening it.

But the cabinet was empty. "Well, they were there yesterday," Sherm grumbled. "Somebody's been messing with my boat!"

Despite the times it misfired, the engine managed to get them back around the island, past the shipwreck and into the sheltered harbor. As they approached the wharf, the engine died. Lying low in the water, the boat glided to safety.

When they reached the dock, Sherm hopped off and tied up the boat securely. "I'm going to have to patch that right away," he said grimly, looking up at the Hardys. "Meantime, run over to that shack across the road over there, will you? You'll find my pump to the right of the door."

Quickly, the Hardys retrieved the pump and brought it back to Sherm, who made quick work of emptying the water from the boat.

"Somebody made that hole with a jigsaw," Joe remarked, bending down and noting the grooves on the sides of the circular hole. "It looks like they went part of the way around the circle and then stopped. It would have been only a matter of time before the rest gave way."

"Sherm, I know lots of crazy things have been

happening, but does anybody on this island have a personal grudge against you?" Frank asked.

Sherm drew a sharp breath. "All right," he said, his jaw tight. "If you kids think you can figure out what's been happening up here when I can't, chew on this. Being sheriff, naturally, I've made some enemies. I wouldn't put it past Nora Stricter or one of her group to cut a hole in my boat. But if you want to know about a personal grudge, old George Hubert is at the top of the list. His family and mine have been enemies since Captain Cook discovered this island. He owns the Makatunk Inn. Well, that inn used to belong to my grandfather. I've been to court with Hubert about it twice in the last ten years. Closed him down once for a week in high season, for health violations. Then he ran against me for sheriff, just to get even. Lost by a mile. Ha! Yes, you might try Hubert, if you're looking for enemies of Sherm Davis."

"Well, Joe?" Frank said, putting his hands on his hips. "I think we have a few places to start. What do you say we get to work?"

"Right," Joe said. "Can you handle the rest of the repairs without us, Sherm?"

Sherm snorted and waved the boys away.

"I guess we can go, Frank," Joe said hastily to his brother. The two of them headed into the village. When they came to the inn, they climbed the steps of the large wraparound porch and went inside.

Frank guessed that the Makatunk Inn must be over a hundred years old. In the lobby, several overstuffed sofas and chairs had been placed around an enormous stone fireplace. Frank and Joe saw a boy of about seventeen carrying a load of folded towels. "Hi, I'm Brian," he said, stopping to greet them. "I saw you guys come off the boat today. Are you staying here at the inn?"

The Hardys told him they were staying at Emma Morton's house and asked if Mr. Hubert was around. "He'll be here at dinnertime," Brian told them. "And if you want to eat here, it's no problem. You don't have to be a guest. We serve family-style, to help people get acquainted. The Makatunk Inn's the island's unofficial gathering place in the evenings."

"Do you know Nora Stricter?" Joe asked.

"Sure. She stays at the inn every year with her group." Brian shifted his load of towels. "I'd better get back to work. See you later. Dinner's at six. You'll hear them ring the bell." With that, he went up the stairs.

"Six is a couple of hours from now," Joe said, checking his watch. "Enough time to shower, change, and get Chet."

"I wonder if he's ready to start eating again," Frank said.

Joe laughed. "Yeah," he said, "because once he's feeling hungry, look out. He'll probably want to make up for lost time!"

Chet was feeling a lot better when the Hardys got back to the house. "You sure get a lot of exercise around here without any telephones," Joe said, when all three boys started heading to town. "In Bayport we would have just phoned to see if you wanted to meet us."

The sun was turning golden over the water when the boys entered the inn. They followed the smells of fresh food to the dining room, a large, airy room overlooking the water. Frank noticed that more than half of the long wooden tables were empty.

The Acorn Society members passed by the Hardys and Chet as they made their way to a table close to the swinging doors of the kitchen. Frank recognized their leader, Nora Stricter, immediately.

When a waitress came out of the kitchen carrying a platter with fish dinners, Nora reacted audibly. "How sad that a person would pollute his or her own body by eating a poor dead creature."

Though the staff looked displeased, Frank noticed that no one said anything to her.

Brian took their order, and as they waited, Joe glanced around the room. The family with children that had come over on the *Maine Maiden* with them were there, too. One of the kids waved to him. At a table far from the others, the Asian couple sat holding hands and smiling at each other.

"Those two really have it bad," Joe joked.

Across the room, Frank noticed the two men who had worn suits on the boat. They were dressed more casually now, in white short-sleeved shirts open at the collar. They looked surprised and slightly uncomfortable when the white-haired couple from the *Maine Maiden* sat down at their table and began chatting with them.

Soon Brian brought a tray of rolls, baked potatoes, buttered corn, and fresh cod to the table the Hardys were sitting at. "Just what the doctor ordered," Chet said, rubbing his hands together.

"Excuse me, guys, but I think this might be a good time to say hello to Nora Stricter," Frank said as they were finishing the meal. He got up and walked over to her table.

"Hello, everybody, I'm Frank Hardy. We passed each other down by the wharf this afternoon. I was very interested in what you told my brother."

"Really?" Nora said, a sudden smile softening her angular features.

"Somebody said you're called the Acorn Society?" he said.

"Yes, that's right, I'm the president," Nora told him. "I formed the group some years ago to teach others to protect the planet. We believe that only when people are respectful of the entity we call earth, will we ensure its, and our own, survival."

"We're explorers," a freckle-faced man next to Nora added. "We're trying to discover how best to travel lightly on the earth."

"That's fascinating," Frank said.

"Perhaps you'd like to join us tomorrow in Cathedral Forest, where the island's giant pines grow. We

31

go there very early to study the forest floor. Morning is the best time for humans to enter woodland areas. At other times, we disturb the feeding patterns of small animals. Did you know that?"

"Why, no, I didn't," Frank said.

"Most people don't," she said. "That's why we have to educate them."

"Well, I . . . okay!" Frank said, giving her a smile and a nod. "My brother and our friend might want to come, too. Is that okay?"

"Wonderful!" Nora said triumphantly. "Meet us there at six. And, please, don't wear sunscreen or insect repellent. They have a disastrous effect on pine trees."

"Six, huh?" Frank echoed faintly.

"The forest is even more beautiful at that hour. Besides, it's never too early to learn about right living, is it?" Nora said with a smile.

Frank nodded, and returned to his table. He felt like kicking himself for agreeing to get up so early. Still, he knew it was probably the best way to investigate Nora Stricter. She certainly had strong opinions about the island.

"Where's Joe?" Frank asked Chet, who was sitting next to Joe's empty chair.

Chet was working on a slice of homemade chocolate cake. "Mphphmgm," he said, pointing to the dining-room door.

"Don't try to explain," Frank said. "I get the idea." Frank walked through the open door into the lobby. There he found Joe talking to an older, white-haired man, who was stoking the fire in the stone fireplace with a load of kindling wood.

"This is my brother, Frank, Mr. Hubert," Joe explained as Frank walked up to them.

Mr. Hubert nodded to Frank without smiling and said, "Your brother's been telling me what happened to Sherm's boat today. Nasty business, very nasty."

Frank knelt down to help with the kindling. It took a lot of wood to make a fire in the inn's huge fireplace. "Mr. Hubert, we've heard there's some bad blood between you and Sherm. Is that true?"

The older man looked surprised. "Now, you don't think I had anything to do with messing up his boat, I hope," he said. "Because that's not how I operate. It's true Sherm and I have feuded, but a man's boat is his livelihood. I know what that means. I suspect the culprits are outsiders looking to make trouble."

"The same outsiders who've been cutting lobster buoys loose and stealing traps?" Joe pressed. "Hasn't this kind of incident been happening for months?"

Hubert grunted and went back to loading the kindling. "I suppose you've got a point there, young man," he said after a while. "There were no outsiders on the island till late April, really. Well, except for Nora. She came out early this year—in March as I recall."

33

Frank looked down at the piece of kindling in his hand. "This is weird," he said, standing up and studying it. "There's something written on this."

"Can you make it out?" Hubert said, looking confused.

Joe peered over Frank's shoulder and read. "It says 'Farley' on it."

"Farley!" Hubert gasped. "How can that be?" He began rummaging through the pile of kindling, a sick look on his face. "Why, this isn't kindling wood at all. It's Farley's lobster traps, and they're all broken up. They must be the ones that were stolen this morning!"

4 A Deadly Discovery

"Now, wait a minute," Mr. Hubert cried, as Joe and Frank turned to look at him. "I didn't do it. I swear! Farley's a friend of mine. Go ask him if you don't believe me."

"Take it easy, Mr. Hubert," Joe said, as the older man awkwardly rose to his feet. "We're not accusing you of anything."

"Anybody could have dropped this wood here," Mr. Hubert insisted. "How was I to know it was someone's broken-up lobster traps? I don't pay close attention to my kindling."

"Who usually brings your wood?" Frank asked.

"Why, Dexter Greenleaf," Mr. Hubert said. "He's the fellow who delivers luggage from the *Maine Maiden.* But I can't believe Dexter would be guilty of anything—"

35

"Guilty of what?" came a voice from behind them. Frank turned to see Dexter standing in the doorway of the inn, frowning. The sleeves of his checkered shirt were rolled up, and he looked like he had put in a hard day's work.

"Dexter," Mr. Hubert said sternly, pointing his finger at the young man. "This isn't kindling! It's Farley's lobster traps. Someone chopped them up. How'd they get here?"

"Don't ask me, Mr. Hubert," Dexter said. He turned to the Hardys and shook his head. "Everybody's going nuts on this island."

"Did you bring this wood to the inn?" Frank asked Dexter.

"Sure I did," Dexter said. "Always do. But I didn't notice anything unusual about it." He turned to Hubert and pointed a menacing finger back at him. "I keep out of trouble, understand? And I got too much to do without stealing anybody's lobster traps. As it is, my day's not finished yet!"

"What kind of business do you have on Makatunk Island after eight at night?" Frank asked.

"None of your business, that's what," Dexter snapped. "Nor anyone else's, neither." Then he stomped out of the lobby and out the door.

Frank wanted to tail him, but he knew that he could never keep up if he were on foot and Dexter was in his truck—especially since it would soon be dark.

"What a mess," Mr. Hubert said. "If we don't put

36

an end to all this trouble, Makatunk will be a deserted island in a year or two."

With that, he excused himself to check on the accommodations for the new arrivals. Frank and Joe said goodbye and stepped outside onto the porch. "It seems to me that somebody *wants* this island deserted," Joe said.

"But why?" Frank asked. He looked around at the idyllic scene. The sky was streaked with vivid orange, red, and purple. On the lawn sloping to the water's edge, a group of teenagers, most of them wearing the T-shirts of Makatunk Inn employees, had gathered to watch the setting sun. Frank noticed Chet was there, too. Frank and Joe went down to join them and quietly filled Chet in on what had just happened. Hoping to pick up some local gossip, they sat down with the group till the sky darkened and the stars came out. But the conversation gave them no new leads.

When the others went inside to play guitar and sing songs by the fireplace, the Hardys and Chet said goodbye and headed back up the hill. "It's a good thing we have our pocket flashlights," Frank said. "I don't think we could find our way back without them—it's so dark."

Soon they were back inside Emma's house, where they lit kerosene lamps. As they got ready for bed, the three discussed the case. "You don't think Mr. Hubert stole the traps, do you?" Joe asked Frank. "I mean, he seems like such a nice guy."

"Joe," Frank said, "think how many nice guys we've helped put in jail."

"I guess you're right," Joe said.

"Anybody want a cookie?" Chet asked from the bedroom doorway, holding out a large bag. "They help you think better."

"Chet, you're amazing," Joe said, laughing. "How can you eat after the dinner you just had?"

"It's easy," Chet said. "You just chew and swallow." With that he bit into a cookie, turned, and went off to his bedroom.

"Anyway," Frank said, returning to the conversation, "who says it was the same person who put the hole in Sherm's boat? I suppose those things could have been done by different people."

"You don't really believe that, do you, Frank?" Joe asked. "This is too small an island to hold a whole gang of criminals."

"True," Frank said thoughtfully. "Well, one thing's for sure. It would only take one bad guy to ruin this entire island. And we've got exactly six days left to find out who it is."

The alarm rang before dawn the next morning. "You can't mean it," Chet complained when Frank knocked on his door to wake him. "We're not really going to traipse around the woods at this hour, are we?"

"We sure are," Frank said. "And remember, no sunscreen or insect repellent."

Chet muttered and grumbled as they got ready to go, but after a quick bowl of cereal, they were soon heading out through the meadow that lay beyond and below Emma's yard. The morning was so cool that Joe could even see his breath in the air.

Frank opened up the map of Makatunk. "We're lucky," he said, "Cathedral Forest is fairly close. Less than two miles."

Wooden signposts led them onto a small path, which brought them to the pine grove. "No cars, no traffic," Joe said as they walked along, "just beautiful silence. I forgot what it's like to be in a forest."

Cathedral Forest was a place of serene beauty. Tall pines reached to the sky, creating dark, cozy shelter even on this sunlit morning. Mosses crept along the ground like a living carpet and covered fallen trees.

"Look at how wide those trees are around," Frank remarked. "That's how you can tell this is a really old forest."

Nora and her group were already there. Most of them had their heads down, and they seemed to be studying the ground intently.

"Good morning, folks," Frank said as they approached.

"How're you doing, everyone?" Joe added.

But their greetings were met with a horrified "Shhhh!" as Nora Stricter pressed her finger to her lips and shot them a sharp look.

Frank, Joe, and Chet exchanged confused looks.

One of the group, a pale woman of about fifty, tiptoed up to the boys and smiled weakly. "We're *listening*," she whispered.

Joe looked at her, then at Frank and Chet and then back to her again. "What are you listening to?" he whispered.

"The forest floor," the woman answered quietly. "We don't want to disturb the balance of those whose home this is. All the sounds of the forest are messages."

"I see," Joe whispered. She tiptoed off to a nearby tree and gazed intently at it.

"What do we do now?" Chet asked impatiently.

"Shhh!" came Nora's swift rebuke.

Joe shrugged but stood quietly by as the Acorn Society members continued to listen. No one spoke, or even moved, except to consult a species identification book or to write a note on the small pads they all carried.

After a while Chet pulled an apple out of his pocket and started munching on it.

"Do you believe this guy?" The man who had sat next to Nora the previous night looked in Chet's direction, then murmured to the woman. Joe wondered what he meant. All Chet was doing was eating an apple.

Oblivious, Chet continued biting until there was nothing left but a tiny core. Then he flung it into a clump of bushes.

Nora caught Chet's action out of the corner of her

40

eye. She straightened up immediately, a look of horror on her face. "Do you realize what you just did?" she asked him in a disapproving whisper.

Chet looked confused. "Ate an apple?" he asked.

Nora gave him a long, hard stare. Another woman hurried to the bushes and fetched the apple core. "Don't worry, Nora, I found it," she said, coming out of the thicket, holding the core as if it were the tail of a dead mouse. "We can take it back with us."

"The first rule of the Acorn Society is no littering," Nora told Chet in a tone of contempt.

"Wait a minute," Frank broke in. "Tossing an apple core into a thicket isn't littering. The core will break down and become soil after a few weeks."

"Is that how you see it?" Nora asked. "How pathetic! You apparently are not looking at the results of that careless action. For instance, suppose a hapless deer wanders by and eats that core?"

"An apple core wouldn't hurt a deer," Joe said.

"Excuse me, my young friend," the freckle-faced man interjected. "An apple core upsets the entire balance of nature in these woods. What if the deer came here seeking apples every day? He wouldn't find them, would he?"

"Or what if another animal was attracted here by the core, an animal who doesn't belong in an old growth forest?" Nora added.

"Okay, okay, I see your point," Chet said. "But aren't you carrying things a little far?"

"How far are you willing to go to save our planet?" Nora asked coldly. "Not very, it seems."

"Look," Chet said, backing down under her assault. "If you want me to take that apple core, I'll be happy to, all right?"

The woman who held the core shook her head disapprovingly. "I'm sorry, but I just don't trust you to dispose of it responsibly."

"I ate the apple, I'll deal with the core, okay?" Chet said, sounding annoyed. He snatched the core from the woman's hand.

"Nora, the bird I was watching just flew off," a member of the group complained.

"I'm afraid there are too many of us gathered here," Nora said, looking at the Hardys and Chet. "Maybe this meeting wasn't a good idea. You boys have a lot to learn. If you are seriously interested, let's get together another time. And until you are properly educated, you should stay out of Cathedral Forest."

She signaled silently to the rest of her group, and they began heading back to the path.

"I don't believe it," Joe muttered as soon as Nora and her group were out of hearing distance.

"They're pretty extreme, all right," Frank said, watching them go. "But I wish I could have questioned Nora about some of the trouble on Makatunk, like the hole in Sherm's boat or Farley's stolen lobster traps. I guess that'll have to wait."

"Listen," Chet said, "I'll catch you later."

"Huh?" Joe said. "Where are you going?"

42

"Back home, to throw away this apple core," he answered.

"Chet!" Joe protested. "You're not really going to walk all the way back to Emma's just to throw away an apple core, are you?"

Chet looked sheepish. "Well, they kind of had a point about upsetting the balance of nature. I mean, suppose a raccoon found it? Or a fox? I'll feel better if I put it in Emma's compost area at least. Meet me in town for lunch, okay? Around twelve-thirty?"

"Do what you have to do, big guy," Frank said with a sigh as Chet took off down the trail. Then he turned to his brother. "Well, getting up at the crack of dawn didn't accomplish anything. I just wish we had even a tiny lead in this case. This is really frustrating."

"I know what you mean, but I also know that we've never been to Makatunk Island before." Joe opened his map and studied it. "Let's check out some sights now, and pick up our investigation this afternoon, okay? We're not far from the cliffs."

"You're on," Frank said. The brothers left Cathedral Forest and continued on the trail, which wound uphill. The area became rockier. Soon they reached a plateau that ended in a sheer cliff. "Wow!" Joe exclaimed, taking in the splendor of the cliff and the surf hundreds of feet below. "Amazing!"

"Let's be careful, though. It's a long way down," Frank cautioned, peering over the edge and down at the sea. Gulls were circling beneath them and the

43

sea crashed rhythmically over the rocky shore. "Hey, look! There are the two men who came over with us on the *Maine Maiden*, Joe."

Joe glanced down and saw one of the men, the light-haired, wiry one, setting up a tripod near the water's edge. "Looks like they're taking pictures."

"That's funny," Frank said. He strained to get a better look. "I don't see any camera on that tripod. Do you?"

"No," Joe said, shielding his eyes from the morning sun. "It's probably in their backpack."

The second man, the dark-haired one with glasses, was carrying what looked like a clipboard. He began pacing away from the camera, taking deliberate steps. "What's he doing?" Joe wondered aloud.

"Let's find out," Frank suggested. He leaned as far over the cliff as safety would let him, and cupped his hands around his mouth. "Hello! Hello!" he shouted down.

The dark-haired man picked up the binoculars that were hanging around his neck. He aimed them upward as Joe and Frank began waving. "He sees us," Joe said. "He's telling his friend."

But instead of waving back, the men immediately started packing up their gear. "What's going on?" Joe asked as he watched them.

"Let's go down there and find out," Frank said.

"Only one problem: How do we get there?" Joe asked. "It's kind of a long drop."

"We'll have to go around by the trail. Hurry!"

By the time the boys got to the bottom, the men were gone. Frank saw their retreating figures a quarter mile in the distance. One of them looked furtively over his shoulder as they hurried away.

"It's as if they're running from us," Frank said, breathing hard from their climb down to the shore. "Come on. Let's catch up with them!"

But by the time the Hardys rounded the corner of the island where the old shipwreck was, the men had disappeared from view. "Rats!" Joe said.

"Don't worry," Frank said. "It's a small island. They're not going anywhere. We'll track them down later."

"This shipwreck is really something," Joe said, gazing at the remains of the hulking cargo ship. Before Frank could say anything Joe was taking off his shoes and socks and rolling up his pants legs. "I'm going to wade out and look it over."

"The map says sightseers climb on the shipwreck at their own risk, Joe," Frank warned. But soon he, too, was wading out to it.

"This is cool," Joe said as he climbed over the edge of the half-submerged ship. One whole end of it was dry and out of the water. "It must have been some storm that drove this baby onto the rocks."

Walking down the slanting surface, the Hardys moved across what once had been the aft end of the ship. Seaweed clung to the area where the boat was submerged, and they could see fish swimming in and out of rusted holes on the far end of the ship. Joe turned back to the aft end, and soon his eyes were drawn to a small brown paper bag neatly resting against the old hull. It seemed too carefully placed to be litter. "Hey, Frank, look what I found," he called out as he opened it.

Inside was a small brown vial of liquid. When Joe turned it around to check out the label, he felt goose bumps rise all over his body.

There, next to a Day-Glo skull and crossbones, were the words: SALMONELLA BACTERIUM. WARNING: POISON. FATAL IF SWALLOWED.

5 Stolen Art

"I think I've discovered why the ship went down," Joe joked grimly. Frank looked up from the rotted porthole he was examining and Joe's expression grew serious. "Get a load of this." He held up the vial so Frank could read the label. If not for the warning, the clear liquid inside would have looked very innocent, unlike the dangerous bacteria it actually contained.

"I suppose there could be a chemist on the island who's doing experiments or something," Frank said.

"Experiments in food poisoning? Not likely," Joe replied. "Anyway, why would a chemist leave a package in a shipwreck?"

"It could be here for someone to pick up," Frank said, examining the vial after Joe handed it to him.

"Maybe if we leave it here and wait around long enough, we could catch the person who's picking it up," Joe said.

"Right," Frank said. "Someone who may try to contaminate food and poison people. This is a lot more dangerous than cutting buoy lines, Joe. Also, if someone dropped this poison off for someone else to pick up, it's got to mean that more than one person is behind the troubles on the island."

"Do you think those two guys left this vial here, Frank? They had to come around this way when we lost them."

Frank nodded. "It's a definite possibility." As he spoke, a family of tourists approached the shipwreck from another trail. "Of course, lots of people come down here. It could have been anybody."

"What do we do now?" Joe asked. "Wait for someone to make the pickup?"

Frank shook his head. "I think we should bring it to Sherm Davis. He's the sheriff, after all, and this vial may be evidence. Besides, we can't let poison fall into the hands of the person who intends to use it."

"But how will we know who's coming to pick it up?" Joe asked. "Like you said, lots of people come to this part of the island."

"I suppose we could leave the package without the vial," Frank suggested.

"Good idea!" Joe said. He took the brown paper bag and put it back where he found it. "I'll wait here. You bring the vial to Sherm."

"Right." Frank pocketed the vial and headed up the rocks off the beach, leaving Joe behind. As he reached the road, he passed the lonely gray and white house that he'd seen from the boat on their way to the island. It was set back a few hundred feet from the sea. Frank remembered that Gabby had told him it belonged to Kent Halliwell, the famous artist.

On the second floor was an open balcony. There, looking out at the sea through binoculars, was a woman with flowing white hair, wearing a purple caftan. Frank recognized the superstar of the art world from the dozens of photos he'd seen of her.

He wondered how long she'd been there and whether she could see the wreck from her balcony. He decided she probably could. Had she seen Joe find the vial of salmonella? Making a quick decision, Frank turned and headed down the path leading to her front door.

He didn't get very far. As he approached, he heard loud barking and growls. In a flash, two enormous black Doberman pinschers with murder in their eyes came bounding down the walkway, racing straight for him. Frank forced himself to act calm as he turned his back on the dogs and walked away.

Luckily, the dogs stopped at the edge of the Halliwell property, though they kept on barking. When he got a safe distance away, Frank looked back at the balcony. Now the binoculars were aimed at him, and the artist seemed to be smiling!

Dogs or no dogs, he'd have a talk with Kent Halliwell before long, Frank decided as he turned back onto the path and continued walking to town. Just then he saw Dexter Greenleaf walking toward him. Dexter was whistling to himself and he seemed to be in a world of his own. Over his arm was a folded green plastic bag, and one of his pockets bulged oddly, as if there were a can in it.

"Dexter, hi," Frank said, startling the workman. Dexter stopped and looked at Frank suspiciously. "Those dogs aren't very friendly, are they," Frank said, hoping to start a conversation with the sullen man.

"Ayeh," Dexter said. "She's got them trained to kill. I've seen them do some damage."

"I was just out at the shipwreck," Frank said, eyeing Dexter for his reaction. "It's cool."

"Ayeh," Dexter replied impassively.

"I bet you never go there, being that you live on the island," Frank went on. "They say most New Yorkers have never been to the Statue of Liberty."

"Oh, I go out to the shipwreck," Dexter told him. "I'm going there right now. You tourists leave trash all over the place and somebody's got to clean it up." With a withering look at Frank, he continued down the rocky path.

Was the plastic bag on his arm there to hide a package? Frank wondered as he watched him go. It was a good thing Joe was there now, ready to observe.

After a fifteen-minute walk, Frank arrived at Sherm's house at the edge of town. He found the sheriff in his front yard, sitting at an outdoor table, repairing a fish net.

"Joe and I found something you should see, Sheriff," he told Sherm, walking over to him.

"Oh?" Sherm said, looking up from the net. "And what might that be?"

Frank pulled out the vial and handed it to the sheriff, explaining how he and Joe had found it.

Sherm studied the vial carefully, with no expression on his face. "You say you were following two men," he said. "Why?"

"They were acting kind of strange," Frank replied. "We had just waved to them. The minute they saw us, they packed up and took off, as if they didn't want us to see what they were doing. That seemed suspicious, so we followed them. But we lost them just before the shipwreck. That's when we found the package there."

"Could be someone left it there to be picked up," Sherm said slowly.

"Exactly," Frank said. "It could have been the two men or anyone else. That's why Joe stayed behind—to see if anyone comes for it."

Sherm nodded, smiling. "You boys are better than I gave you credit for. Keep up the good work."

"There's more," Frank said. "I'm pretty sure that Kent Halliwell saw everything, too. She was on her balcony looking through binoculars. She might have seen whoever dropped off the vial. I wanted to talk to her, but her dogs chased me away."

"Ayeh, she keeps her dogs mean to scare away tourists," Sherm said. "Ms. Halliwell likes her privacy, and she doesn't get much of it."

"I think we should talk to her," Frank said.

"I'll do that," Sherm said. "And I'll put this away for safekeeping, too." He tucked the vial in his shirt pocket and patted it.

"Hey, how's your boat?" Frank asked.

"Oh, it'll be all right once the engine dries out," Sherm said. "I patched up the hole for the moment. As long as I don't push it too hard, or take it out in a storm, it'll last."

"One last thing," Frank said, "We found Mr. Farley's lobster traps. They were in pieces on Mr. Hubert's kindling pile. And Dexter delivered that kindling to the inn."

"Doesn't mean Dexter stole the traps," Sherm said. "Anybody could have piled that stuff on top. Even Hubert. You don't know him," Sherm added darkly. "He's capable of anything, I tell you."

"That may be," Frank said. "But I just passed Dexter on the trail. He was on his way to the shipwreck."

Sherm looked at Frank. "I'm a sheriff, not a prosecutor," he said. "Suspicions don't mean anything unless I can prove them. Now, I knew Dexter as a boy, and he had his problems. But a man has a right to make a fresh start. Believe me, if I find he's guilty, I'll arrest him. Till then, I'm not saying another word. Let me handle things in my own way, son. You and your brother just enjoy your time on Makatunk. Take care now."

With that, the sheriff fixed his concentration on his net, and Frank stood there awkwardly for a moment. "See you, then," he said. He walked back to the path. Sherm's lack of cooperation was unsettling. And if he was working on the case, Frank thought, he had a strange way of doing it—sitting in front of his house fixing a fish net.

Frank glanced at his watch. It was just past noon, time to meet Chet at the coffee shop. He started on the path and glanced quickly back at Sherm's house.

What he saw there made him freeze. Dexter Greenleaf was running like a deer through some bushes behind Sherm's yard! Had he doubled back and been spying on Frank and the sheriff? Frank felt certain he'd heard every word of their conversation.

Gritting his teeth, Frank hurried to town. He was going to get to the truth about Dexter, whatever it took. There had to be a reason Sherm was so closemouthed about the handyman.

"Over here, Frank!" Chet called out from the back of the coffee shop when Frank entered. Chet was already working on a submarine sandwich.

"Have the waitress wrap it up, Chet," Frank told him. "And get two more to go, for me and Joe."

Frank filled in Chet on the morning's events as the waitress wrapped the sandwiches. Frank paid for his and Joe's. "Give this one to Joe," he said, handing the sandwich to Chet. "I'll meet you guys at the shipwreck as soon as I can," he said.

"Where are you going?" Chet asked, surprised.

"To the gallery," Frank told him. "I want to check out some of Kent Halliwell's paintings. She's the island's most famous attraction. Maybe I'll get some more leads over at the gallery."

Frank wolfed down his sandwich, then hurried across the road to the white clapboard building with bright purple trim. When he entered the storefront gallery, he saw the red-haired woman who had been sweeping the day before, sitting behind a desk. She was reading the *Bar Harbor Times*. She looked to be in her late twenties.

"Hello," she said. "May I help you?"

"I'll be honest," Frank confessed, "I came to see if you had any Kent Halliwells, although I know I can't afford to buy one."

"You're a browser, that's okay," the woman said with a smile. "I'm Ilsa Crawford, the owner. And I like browsers. We have them here all the time."

Her soft European accent, thick French braid, and mandarin-style silk jacket gave the gallery owner a sophisticated, international flair. But the nicest thing about her was her friendly, open manner. She was going to be easy to talk to, Frank thought.

"Great," he said. "I'm Frank Hardy."

"Well, Frank, you're very lucky," Ilsa told him. "I just received four new oils from Kent last night. They're still in the back, though, because my assistant wasn't here this morning to hang them."

"That's great! I'm a real fan," Frank continued.

"Most people are," Ilsa replied with a little laugh. "If Kent did finger paintings I could still sell them. I think it's the way she uses color. Her work just makes people feel good."

"Do you know her personally?" Frank asked.

"Yes, I've known her for years," Ilsa told him. "In fact, my father was one of the first to sell her work when he ran the gallery. He's retired now."

"This morning, I thought I'd try to get her autograph, so I went out to her house," Frank said. "Unfortunately, I didn't meet her, only her dogs."

Ilsa shuddered. "Oh, yes, Fritz and Franz," she said. "Intimidating little pups, aren't they?"

"I'm afraid so," Frank had to admit.

"Well, congratulations on surviving," Ilsa said with a grin. "Come on into the back room and I'll show you the new arrivals."

Frank followed her into the small back room, which was crowded with paintings and prints. There was an exit on one wall and a door to a rest room on the other. Ilsa flipped through a particular stack once, twice, three times, with a confused look on her face. When she straightened up, the look was of panic. "They're not here," she said.

"Are you sure?" Frank asked.

"Yes, I'm sure. I put them here myself!"

"Then there's only one explanation," Frank said, staring at the gallery owner.

"I'm afraid you're right," Ilsa said, her voice hoarse with dread. "The new Halliwell paintings must have been stolen!"

6 Poisoned?

"Please don't panic," Frank told the distraught gallery owner. "Are you sure the paintings didn't get moved?"

"Yes, I'm sure," Ilsa said immediately. "Kent delivered them personally, and I put them behind this stack until I could hang them."

Frank walked over to the back entrance of the gallery and studied the lock on the door. "Is this all the security you have on this door?" he asked. He opened it and examined the edge.

"Yes," Ilsa confessed. "After all, we've never had a theft here, not in all the years my father ran the gallery, nor since I took it over. Makatunk Island has always been known for the honesty of its people. Or should I say, it *was* known for it."

57

"You said you saw the paintings this morning. Then they had to be taken today," Frank said.

"Yes, but how could it be?" Ilsa protested. "I was here the whole time!"

"My brother and I saw you sweeping out front."

"Oh, yes, I do that every day."

"Who visited the shop this morning?" Frank asked. "Do you remember?"

The gallery owner shrugged helplessly. "Honestly, I wasn't paying attention. And since I keep some prints and posters back here for sale, people come and go freely from this room. I wouldn't know what they do when they're back here."

"Think, Ilsa. You must remember someone from this morning," Frank asked.

"Well, there was an Asian couple. They bought a print, in fact. A woodcut by Merry Haverstraw." Ilsa took a deep breath as she tried to remember more. "Sherm came in to say hello, and we talked awhile. Oh, he went in the back to use the restroom. I'll have to get in touch with him right away to report this, won't I?" Ilsa pressed her lips together, thinking. "Let's see, Nora Stricter came by around lunchtime. Do you know her?"

"Yes," Frank said. "What about Dexter Greenleaf? Was he here?"

The gallery owner looked perplexed. "Dexter is here every day. I pay him to haul my trash."

"And, of course, he was in this room because it's where you keep the trash barrel," Frank said, pointing to a clean white plastic container.

58

"Right," Ilsa said.

"How about two men, in their thirties, or late twenties? One with glasses?"

"Not that I recall," Ilsa said.

"Did any of the people you remember seem anxious or nervous in any way?"

"Not really. I chatted with some of them. But I was also reading the paper. I guess I'm in the habit of trusting people," she said sadly.

Frank understood how she felt. It was a shame that a beautiful place like Makatunk Island was being spoiled by crime. "How much were the paintings worth?" he asked.

"A few thousand dollars," she replied. "But it isn't just the money. If art is stolen from my gallery, artists won't give me their work to sell. That will put me right out of business."

"It could even go further than that," Frank pointed out. "Art is big business on Makatunk Island, isn't it?"

"Oh, yes," she replied. "A lot of tourists come just to buy artwork and look at the artists' homes."

"Then if the artists leave, so might the tourists."

"I hadn't thought of that," the gallery owner said. "Do you think someone is trying to destroy the tourist trade?"

"I think if we find out who stole these paintings we might discover who's responsible for the other crimes, too." Frank said. "And then we'll find out their motives. Any ideas on where to start?"

Ilsa's face brightened suddenly. "No, but I just

59

thought of something! The *Maine Maiden* doesn't return to the mainland till tomorrow morning. The paintings must still be on the island! Maybe they can still be recovered."

"Good thinking," Frank said.

Ilsa's face fell. "Of course, I've still got to tell Kent what happened. She won't like it a bit. Knowing her, she may even blame me."

"That wouldn't be fair," Frank protested.

"Great artists aren't known for being fair," Ilsa replied. "They're known for their passion."

"Can I go over there with you?"

"Would you? That would be great," Ilsa said, looking relieved. "Kent can be frightening when she's angry."

Ilsa locked up her shop, and they headed down the path, arriving at the artist's home in about twenty minutes.

"Kent!" Ilsa called. "It's me! Ilsa!"

Soon the famous artist appeared, her binoculars still around her neck. She walked out of the house and strode down the walkway to meet them.

Ilsa looked nervous as she faced her. "I'm afraid I have terrible news," she said. "The paintings you brought to the gallery last night have been stolen."

Kent Halliwell's large green eyes widened. "What happened?" she demanded.

Ilsa filled her in as best she could, as the artist listened intently. "I know you must be angry," Ilsa concluded. "And I just want you to know how sorry I am."

"I hope they were insured," Frank interjected.

"Who are you?" the artist asked, turning to Frank. "And why are you here?"

"This is Frank Hardy, Kent," Ilsa told her. "He was there when I discovered the theft, and he's been very kind to me."

The artist stared at Frank, as if she were assessing him. He must have met with her approval because when she answered him, the harshness of her tone had softened. "Yes, the paintings were insured," she said. "But I don't care about that. I came to Makatunk to escape the ways of the world. Now it seems there is no haven to be found anywhere. I thought I would be left in peace on this island. It is the only way I can work!"

"Ms. Halliwell," Frank began, "my brother and I are trying to get to the bottom of the problems on this island. Earlier today, when we found something at the shipwreck, I noticed you standing on your balcony looking our way. Did you happen to see two men on the wreck, before we got there?"

"Well, yes, I did. I assumed they were photographers because they carried a tripod. One man stayed on the beach and the other waded out to the wreck. They were there just before you and the blond fellow," she answered.

"That's my brother Joe," Frank explained.

"But that's hardly unusual," the artist replied. "Many tourists explore the wreck, even though they are warned not to."

"You've been very helpful," Frank told her,

excited by the confirmation of what he had already suspected—that the two men he and Joe had seen earlier were connected to the bottle of salmonella bacteria found at the shipwreck. Turning to Ilsa, he added, "I'd better go find my brother. See you later." Waving goodbye, he headed down to the shipwreck. He found Joe and Chet standing on the beach, skimming rocks into the surf.

"At last!" Joe said when he saw Frank. "Where have you been? Nobody's come anywhere near that package."

"Not even Dexter?" Frank asked.

"Dexter?" Joe repeated. "No, he hasn't been here."

"I had a feeling you'd say that," Frank said, remembering Dexter running from Sherm's backyard.

"Could it be that whoever was going to make the pickup backed off when he saw you two?" Frank asked.

"Hey, I'm insulted!" Chet said. "Did you think we were standing out here in the open the whole time? We've been hidden in the trees over there for the last hour!"

"Honestly, Frank," Joe said. "We only gave up about ten minutes ago."

"All right," Frank said. "I guess no one's going to show. Let's pack it in for now, and go back to the house."

* * *

That evening the boys made their way down to the inn for dinner. As they settled down at a table, Mr. Hubert stopped by. "Farley caught an eight-foot-long halibut," he said with a smile. "I recommend it tonight."

"I kind of admire vegetarians," Chet confessed as Brian came over to take their order. "But there's no way I'm going to miss out on fresh halibut."

"Me, neither," Frank agreed.

"I'm not crazy about fish," Joe admitted. "I think I'll try the vegetarian platter."

Just then the two men Frank and Joe had seen at the shipwreck appeared at the dining-room door.

"Suddenly, I'm feeling extremely friendly," Joe said, his eyes fixed on them. "Mind if I invite those two to sit at our table?"

"Good idea," Frank said. "And, Chet, once they're here, perhaps you'll be able to entertain them with some magic tricks."

"Huh? Magic tricks?" Chet said, looking confused for a second. "Oh, I get it. You want me to keep them occupied while you—"

"Don't say it," Frank advised. He knew Chet had figured out that this would be a perfect time for the Hardys to search the two men's rooms.

Joe got up from the table and boldly walked up to the two men.

"Hi! Remember me from the ferry over here? I'm Joe Hardy," he said, giving them each a friendly handshake. The men looked at Joe a bit suspiciously, but he continued. "That's my brother Frank, and our friend Chet Morton. Come on over and sit with us. We've got plenty of room!"

The men exchanged uncomfortable glances, but Joe didn't leave much room for them to refuse. "What're your names?" Joe asked, ushering them over to the table.

"I'm Glenn Carter," the thin and wiry man with the sandy hair said. He had a sunburn on his cheeks and neck.

"Bob D'Amico," said the dark-haired, heavy-set man with brown eyes and glasses.

"Well, Glenn, and Bob, meet Frank and Chet. What brings you to Makatunk Island?" Joe asked.

There was an awkward pause, and once again the men looked at each other, which Joe thought odd. "Oh, the outdoors," D'Amico said. "Fishing, hunting, all that stuff."

"That's right," Glenn said.

"Glenn, Bob, what will you have?" Frank asked, signaling for Brian to come take their order.

"You don't have London broil by any chance, do you?" the wiry man asked the waiter, who shook his head. "Prime rib? Lamb chops?"

"Just halibut, or a vegetarian platter," Brian told them. "There aren't enough people for the chef to make a lot of different dishes."

"Well, I guess I'll take the vegetarian platter," Bob announced. "It sounds very good."

"Uh, me, too," Glenn told Brian.

"Three veggie platters and two halibut for this table," Brian repeated. "Coming right up."

"How do you like the inn?" Joe asked. "Are you in one of the rooms with a view of the ocean?"

"Yes," Bob said. "It's very nice."

"Is this your first time here?" Joe pressed, trying to sound like a friendly fellow tourist.

When they nodded, Frank stood up. "I'll be right back," he said. "I need to wash up."

"I'll go with you, Frank," Joe said. "Oh, Bob, Glenn," he continued as he rose and joined Frank. "You're in luck. Chet's aunt owns a place here on Makatunk. He can tell you all about the island."

"It all started with the Makatunk Indians," Chet began, launching into what promised to be a detailed history of the island. Glenn and Bob didn't look exactly enthralled, but they sat and listened anyway as they waited for their dinner.

"Good old Chet," Frank murmured as soon as he and Joe got out of the dining room. "He'll keep them occupied for a while."

"Let's see, if they face the ocean, at least we know which side of the inn they're on," Joe said. "But how do we find out which are their rooms?"

"Over here," Frank said, leading his brother to the desk in the lobby. He opened the registration book.

"G. Carter, room 227, and Bob D'Amico, room 229," Frank said quietly. "Easy!" The brothers hurried up the stairs at the end of the first-floor hallway.

"Getting in won't be hard, either," Frank said. "Not with these old locks." He produced the Swiss Army knife that he carried everywhere, inserted it in the edge of the doorjamb of room 227, and jiggled the knife and the handle.

"Presto!" The door swung open and the Hardys slipped inside. It was simply furnished, with a bed, an antique oak dresser, a rocking chair, and a small bedside table with a kerosene lamp on it. But nothing in Glenn Carter's room gave them a clue about what he and his friend were doing on the island. "Could it be that they're just here on vacation, like they said?" Joe wondered aloud as they went back into the hallway and opened the door to room 229.

"I guess anything's possible," Frank said dubiously. The second room was as neat as the first, although some of the furniture was different. The boys made their way quickly to the spindly wooden desk in front of the large shuttered window. Frank knelt down and checked the drawers as Joe shuffled through the few papers on top of the desk.

"Look, Frank," Joe said, holding out a spreadsheet to his brother. Frank stood up after wrestling unsuccessfully with a stuck drawer. The heading on the paper read RHI. The page had a list of expenses. One item stood out immediately—several hundred dollars for outdoor gear, including archery equipment, hunting rifles, and fishing poles. "If these two guys are on vacation, why have they charged this stuff to their company?" Joe asked.

Then Frank noticed an even stranger item—laboratory supplies. "Could this refer to salmonella bacteria?"

"Hmmm," Joe murmured.

"Come on, Joe, we'd better get back," Frank said. "They may wonder where we've gone. But I think we're finally getting someplace."

"Yes, but where?" Joe wondered aloud.

Downstairs, the room was filled with the aroma of fresh halibut. Frank noticed that Nora and her group looked extremely upset. "Fish murderers," Nora Stricter muttered audibly when one of the waitresses appeared with another platter of fresh fish.

When their dinners came, Glenn and Bob ate as if they were in a speed-eating contest. "Nice talking to you fellas," Bob said as they stood up from the table. "Time for us to turn in. We're going hunting tomorrow and we want to get an early start."

"See you around," Chet told them. But as soon as they were out of earshot, he added, "That's strange. There is no hunting on Makatunk Island. Everyone knows that."

"RHI, RHI," Frank murmured, "What can those letters stand for?" But before any of them could venture a guess, Chet suddenly doubled over.

"My stomach!" he moaned.

"I feel sick," said a woman at a table behind them. Her companion, too, was clutching his stomach.

Frank looked around the room. A number of

people seemed to be having the same problem. He was wondering if there was something he could do to help them, when an invisible knife seemed to slice through his belly. "What the—Joe, I'm sick, too," he said, bending over.

"Let me get you two outside for some fresh air," Joe said. He pushed himself away from the table and came around to help Frank and Chet.

Joe took them each by the elbow and helped them out onto the porch. Chet's face was pale, and he was groaning in pain. "Thanks, Joe," Frank managed to say. The searing pain in his gut made him wonder if he was going to pass out.

Just then, a man appeared, leaning over Chet with a small flashlight that he had taken from his pocket. "I'm Dr. Mendez, a friend of Mr. Hubert's. It's a good thing I decided to have dinner at the inn tonight," the doctor said, peering into Chet's eyes. "Hmmm." He checked Frank's eyes and then turned to Joe. "You ate the vegetarian platter, didn't you?" he asked Joe.

"Yes," Joe said. "How did you know?"

"I had it, too, fortunately. It seems everyone who ate the fish is sick as a dog," Dr. Mendez said. "That halibut was tainted."

"Tainted?" Joe said, swallowing hard. "Tainted with what?"

"There's no doubt about it," the doctor replied grimly. "Looks to me like this is a serious outbreak of salmonella poisoning."

7 Cave-in!

"Salmonella!" Joe repeated. His clear eyes met Frank's glazed ones. "How bad is it, Doctor?" Joe asked.

"I don't know yet," the doctor said. "Salmonella is most serious among children and older people. The more bad food you eat, the worse the infection. Fortunately, it responds well to antibiotics. I keep a good supply on the island."

Pointing to Chet, the doctor added, "This young man seems particularly hard hit." Chet's face looked puffy and his eyes were closed.

"He ate two helpings of fish," Joe explained.

"Ooohhh," Chet moaned. "I'll never eat fish again!"

"There were children in the dining room," Joe told the doctor. "I hope they're okay."

"I'm just going to run over to my office and pick up some supplies. I'll be back in a jiffy," the doctor said. "If you see Mr. Hubert, please tell him where I've gone." With that, the doctor hurried away from the inn.

"Joe," Frank said, still holding his stomach with one hand, "get over to Sherm's right away. See if that vial is still there!"

"Are you sure you'll be all right?" Joe asked, not wanting to leave Frank and Chet when they were sick.

"Yes, I'm sure," Frank said.

"Okay," Joe said, getting up. "I'll be right back. Stay right here."

"Don't worry," Frank said. "We're not going anywhere. Ooohhh . . ."

Joe was off in a flash, running down the road as the sun set over the island. When he got to Sherm's house, he found the sheriff by the front door. The lock on the door was broken, and the frame was shattered.

"Somebody forgot to knock," Sherm said, as Joe came up beside him.

"What happened?" Joe asked.

"Ilsa Crawford told me about the missing oils. I went over to Dexter's to ask him about them, and about Farley's lobster traps. But he wasn't there. When I got home, I found the door like this."

"Maybe Dexter was here, breaking down your door to get to that salmonella," Joe said.

70

"What?" Sherm looked at Joe in astonishment. "What makes you think it's missing?"

"Just a wild guess," Joe said dryly. "There are dozens of sick people over at the inn, and the doctor says it's salmonella."

"Let's have a look," Sherm said grimly. He led Joe into the room off the kitchen and opened the drawer. "It's gone," he said. "And here I was thinking it was strange that they broke down the door but didn't steal anything."

"Frank told me that after he left your house today he saw Dexter spying on you," Joe said.

"Well, that would explain things, wouldn't it?" Sherm said, stroking his chin. "I guess I didn't realize how much worse he'd gotten since he was sent away."

"Sent away?" Joe repeated. "What do you mean?"

Sherm shifted his gaze away from Joe. "That just slipped out," he admitted. "I promised his mother I wouldn't tell anybody. I can't . . ."

"Sheriff," Joe said forcefully, "you've got to tell us what you know!"

Sherm shook his head. "Sorry, I can't," he said. "I made a solemn promise."

"Let us talk to his mother then," Joe said.

Sherm sighed deeply. "Dexter's mother passed away six months ago, Joe," he said. "But you boys can find out about Dexter if you've a mind to. Meanwhile, I'd better get over to the inn and see if I can help. There'll be time for me to talk to Dexter. He's not going anywhere, after all."

"He'd better not," Joe said under his breath. He was sure now that Dexter was behind things. Whatever secret Dexter was hiding, it was serious enough that his mother had made Sherm swear not to tell.

Joe knew what Frank would say: "A man is innocent until proven guilty." But Joe wasn't going to rest until he'd found out Dexter's dark secret.

Joe and Sherm headed for the inn. The guests who had eaten in the dining room were up in their rooms, lying down. The staff had its hands full, bringing clean laundry, hot tea, and other things up to the sick. Luckily, none of the staff was sick because they had not had a chance to eat and hadn't tasted the fish.

The Acorn Society members were helping out, too. Joe noticed that Nora Stricter had a smug look on her face, and he overheard her remark to one of her group that now maybe people would pay more attention to her teachings. He wondered if the salmonella could have been hers.

Joe found Frank and Chet sitting on the porch steps. Chet was sweating, but Frank looked a little better. "How are you fellas going to get home?" Sherm asked, joining the boys.

"Somebody went to get Dexter," Frank said, his voice tight. "He's coming with his truck."

"Great," Joe said. "I've got a few questions to ask that guy."

Just as Joe said the words, Dexter arrived in his

beat-up pickup. Joe helped Frank onto the back, while Dexter helped Chet, who lay down next to Frank. "Bad fish, eh?" Dexter asked Sherm.

"I guess so, Dexter," Sherm said thoughtfully. He looked at Dexter intently. "I went over to your place a while ago. You were out."

"Ayeh," Dexter said, not offering any explanation of where he'd been. He got in the cab of the truck and shut the door. Joe hopped in on the passenger side, and with a wave to Sherm, they were on their way to Hawk's Hill Road.

"So, where were you when Sherm came to your house?" Joe asked Dexter, determined to get some answers.

Dexter kept his eyes on the road. "Working," he said. "I've got a lot of jobs around here. Any problem with that?"

"As a matter of fact, I've got a lot of problems," Joe challenged, "And I'd like to talk to you about them."

"I'm not much for talking," Dexter said, pulling over and stopping the truck. "Here's your house. I'll help your friends inside." They got out and Joe helped Chet and Frank upstairs to their beds. "That'll be ten dollars," Dexter told Joe when he came back downstairs.

Joe shook his head in amazement. "Don't you ever do anything just to be nice?"

"I've got to make a living," Dexter told him at the door. "It's not my fault your friends are sick."

"Is that so?" Joe shot back, stepping out onto the

porch. He pulled a ten-dollar bill from his pocket and paid the workman.

"'Night," Dexter said, getting into his truck and pulling away.

As he turned to go inside, Joe noticed a note stuck under the door. If it had been there before, he hadn't seen it. He picked it up and read the crudely written scrawl: *I KNOW WHERE THE PAINTINGS ARE. MEET ME—ALONE—AT THE OLD WEBSTER SHACK.*

Joe bounded up the stairs to the bedroom. Frank, looking a bit pale, was sitting up in bed.

"How're you feeling?" Joe asked him.

"Much better," Frank said, managing a smile. "I never did finish my dinner, thank goodness."

"Check out this note," Joe said, passing it to him.

Frank read it and looked up at Joe. "Let's go," he said, throwing the coverlet back. "I remember seeing the Webster Shack on the map. It's near the old cemetery, off Clover Bee Road."

"Wait a minute!" Joe stopped him. "You're supposed to stay in bed for twenty-four hours. Doctor's orders!"

"Never mind that," Frank said, standing up and reaching for his jeans. "This is important!"

Joe knew he couldn't stop him, so he let Frank finish dressing. After checking in on Chet, who was already asleep, the two brothers left the house, flashlights in hand. "We take Hawk's Hill Road to the end and turn left on Clover Bee. The Webster Shack should be right there."

Five minutes later they were shining their lights on a dilapidated ruin of a house. Its roof sagged so badly in the middle that it looked as if it might collapse at any moment. It had obviously been abandoned a very long time ago. "This has got to be the place," Frank said. "Let's go in."

"Hello?" Joe called out as they entered the shack, which still smelled strongly of old fish. "Anybody here?" Only silence answered him.

Frank shone his flashlight around. "Look, Joe!" he cried out. "The paintings!"

The Halliwell paintings were clearly visible leaning against one of the rotting wooden beams. Joe shone his flashlight on them, and gasped. "Somebody's slashed them!" he said. "They're ruined!"

Frank opened his mouth to say something, but he never got the chance. At that moment, there was a low groan of wood, then the sound of wood splintering.

"Frank!" Joe shouted. "We've got to get out of here! The whole place is coming down!"

Joe grabbed Frank and turned for the door, but it was too late. With a sharp crack, the roof caved in right on top of them!

8 Moving Targets

Everything was black. Frank ached all over. He felt like he had been hit by a wrecking ball. His head was throbbing, and he felt blood on the fingers of his right hand. "Joe?" he called out. "Joe, are you all right?"

There was no answer. A horrible feeling of dread came over Frank. He pushed aside the pieces of rotting wood that were pinning him to the ground, and slowly struggled to his feet. Above him, the stars were plainly visible where the roof of the building had been.

"Joe?" he called again, hunting for the flashlight that had been knocked out of his hand. But he couldn't find it. Only when the moon appeared out of some clouds was there any light.

Frank froze when he caught sight of a hand sticking out from under a beam. It wasn't moving.

"Joe!" Frank cried, rushing over and using all the strength left in him to push the beam aside. Joe was covered with so much debris, Frank couldn't imagine there was any air for breathing.

Finally, Frank managed to dig out his brother and pull him into a relatively clear space. "Joe! Are you all right?" he asked anxiously, kneeling at his side.

Joe's eyes slowly flickered open. "Ooohhhh," he moaned softly. "What happened?"

"The roof came down, that's what happened," Frank said. "Are you okay?"

"I . . . I heard you calling, but I was jammed under a beam," Joe said, trying to sit up. "I think I'm okay now."

"We're lucky the wood was so rotten," Frank said. "If the termites hadn't chewed out the center of these beams, making them lighter, we'd both be dead by now."

Frank got up and looked around the wreckage in the moonlight. Something caught his eye, and he knelt back down. "Hey! There are saw marks on this beam," he said, feeling the wood with his fingers. "This was no accident. I think someone lured us here to try to get rid of us!"

"That's good," Joe said. "We must be getting close to figuring out the mystery. Otherwise, why would they bother?"

"We'd better be a lot more careful from now on,"

Frank said. "Or we'll end up like the Halliwell paintings," he added grimly.

Joe got up and brushed the dust off his clothes. "Are you sure you're okay?"

"My arm hurts, but it's nothing serious," Frank said. "How about you?"

"My leg is cut and I'm a little dizzy, but, hey— I'm alive," Joe answered. "How lucky can I get?"

"Come on," Frank said. "Let's get home." The two brothers limped back up the hill to Emma's with only the light of the moon to guide them. Chet was still sound asleep. After Frank and Joe cleaned their cuts and checked their bruises they carefully lay down. As soon as Frank's head hit his pillow a wave of exhaustion crashed over him. The shock of what had happened had made him forget his aching stomach. He heard his brother's slow breathing and he knew Joe was already sleeping. Despite his fatigue, the events of the day whirled around in his head. Finally, after tossing and turning uncomfortably, he managed to fall asleep.

The next morning, Frank awoke feeling much better. The pain in his stomach was almost all gone, and once he bandaged his arm, it hardly bothered him at all. He hoped the others were recovered as well.

"My leg could be worse," Joe said as he got out of bed. He limped a little as he got dressed. "But if somebody thinks they can stop me by dropping a roof on my head, they'd better think again!"

The two brothers went into Chet's room. "How're you feeling, buddy?" Frank asked, sitting down on Chet's bed.

"Terrible," Chet moaned, his eyes still closed. "You guys go have a good time. I'm not moving. Some vacation this is!"

"We'll check in on you later," Frank said. "Let's go, Joe. We can grab some breakfast at the coffee shop after we see Ilsa."

Frank and Joe headed down the hill to the gallery, where Ilsa Crawford was just opening up shop. Her pretty face fell when she heard what had happened at the Webster Shack. "Thank goodness you two are all right," she said. "But it's horrible that the paintings were destroyed. That might make Kent leave Makatunk forever, and that would be a disaster!"

Ilsa led them outside, and locked up the gallery. "I want Kent to hear about it from me before she hears about it from anyone else. And I just hope whoever did this is caught—fast."

"We're going to work on that right away," Joe said. "Come on, Frank. Let's go see Sherm."

The brothers ate a quick breakfast at the coffee shop, then headed to the sheriff's house. Sherm greeted them in the yard with a smile, but his grin vanished when they told him what had happened the night before. "It's time to call in the state police, Sherm," Frank said. "My brother and I could have been murdered last night."

79

"I'm not going to do that," Sherm insisted. "That would be the worst thing possible. If the papers got hold of this, it'd be the end of everything up here."

"I bet a lot of tourists are already packing their bags," Joe said. "That is, if they've recovered from the salmonella poisoning!"

Sherm pulled at his lower lip, and scratched his cheek. "Maybe if I go to the mainland and talk things over with the police there, quiet like, I'll get some backup and suggestions on how to proceed," he said.

"Did you follow Dexter last night?" Frank asked.

"Tried to," Sherm said. "He gave me the slip when he rode you boys home. By the time I got halfway up Hawk's Hill Road, his truck passed me coming down. I thought I saw him around the old Webster Shack, but then I lost sight of him again."

"The Webster Shack!" Joe gasped, and looked at his brother. "Frank, it's got to be Dexter! He's been everywhere there's been an incident."

"Well, I can't arrest him without better proof." Sherm looked down at his watch. "If I'm going to see my boss on the mainland, I'd better hurry. The *Maine Maiden* leaves in twenty minutes."

Frank and Joe went down to the dock with the sheriff, arriving as the *Maine Maiden*'s gangplank was being set out. Frank noticed the family with children he'd seen coming over. The parents looked pale, but the children were full of energy.

"We're cutting our vacation short," the man told Frank after they exchanged a greeting. "My wife is terrified that there might be another food-poisoning incident."

"It's a good thing we hate fish!" their oldest son, a boy of about ten, piped up.

Sherm walked over to the Hardys and put a hand on Frank's shoulder. "You boys might as well run along now. I'll see you in the morning, when the *Maine Maiden* comes back in."

Frank and Joe said goodbye to Sherm and turned away from the *Maine Maiden* as the ferry blasted its final boarding call.

"Come on, Joe, let's take a walk," Frank suggested. "We've got to think this case through, and I think better when I'm in motion."

"What's to think about?" Joe asked. "Everything points to Dexter! He's obviously the one making the trouble around here. You heard Sherm say how Dexter was near the Webster Shack last night. And remember, he was at the art gallery the morning the Halliwell paintings were taken, too. He's always where the trouble is."

"That's all true, Joe, but I have a big problem with Dexter being the culprit," Frank said, frowning. "What's his motive?"

"What's Dexter's motive? Well, uh . . ." Joe pressed his lips together in thought. After a moment, he said reluctantly, "I see what you mean. I'm not sure he has a motive."

"What would Dexter possibly stand to gain by the tourist industry on this island going up in smoke?" Frank challenged. "And why would he want to see the art galleries put out of business? It doesn't make sense. Dexter depends on the economy of this island to live."

"He sure seems like a hard worker," Joe noted as they wandered through town, toward Hawk's Hill Road. "The guy's always trying to get a dollar."

"Now, Nora Stricter," Frank said. "There's someone with a motive. She'd obviously love to destroy the fishing industry. The way she feels about people eating fish is pretty clear. And wouldn't she want to get rid of the tourists? They interfere with the natural balance of the island, after all."

"But," countered Joe, "the tourist business is a good way for her to get her message to people. Remember—she wants to educate everyone. Besides, why would she try to destroy the art business?"

Suddenly they were startled by a familiar voice behind them.

"Well, look who's here! How do you like Makatunk, lads?"

Frank and Joe spun around and saw Gabby Smith, the captain of the *Maine Maiden*, walking up to them. "Why aren't you on your ship?" Frank

82

asked, smiling. Behind Gabby, Frank saw the ship moving away from the island toward the Maine coast.

"Now that I'm getting older, my wife wants me to cut down on my trips," the captain explained. "I've trained my first mate to captain the boat three afternoons a week. Where are you off to, lads? The cliffs? It's a beautiful day for them."

"We're just walking, right now," Frank confessed. "Trying to sort things out. There've been some serious problems since we arrived."

"I was on the mainland for a few days, but I heard all about it from George Hubert this morning when I came in," the captain said, falling in step with them and shaking his head sadly. "Food poisoning, stolen art. Pretty nasty business."

"Gabby, it seems wherever there's trouble, Dexter Greenleaf is somewhere to be found," Frank said, hoping the friendly captain loved to talk on land as much as he did at sea. "What do you know about him?"

"Dexter Greenleaf, ayeh, he's had his share of trouble," the captain said. "You know his mother died about six months ago. Dexter came back to the island shortly after that. He served his time and was a free man."

"You mean he was in prison?" Joe asked, his eyes widening.

"Detention center for youth," Gabby corrected him. "He served a six-year sentence for assault with a deadly weapon, or some such. Though if you ask me, the punishment was worse than the crime."

"Why? What was he in for?" Frank prompted.

"Mind you, I wasn't there when it happened, and neither was anyone else. But apparently, young Dexter had some sort of run-in with Sherm Davis. He got so upset he took a rifle and went to Sherm's house looking for trouble."

"Sherm? The crime was against Sherm?" Frank said, amazed.

"That's why it went so hard on Dexter, Sherm being sheriff and all," Gabby went on. "Just about broke Barbara Greenleaf's heart, too. She pleaded with Sherm not to press charges. Not only did she love her boy, but even then she depended on the lad to help earn money. Dexter has been doing odd jobs since his father died when he was eleven. He always was a good worker."

"Why was Dexter so mad at Sherm?" Joe asked.

"That I don't rightly know," Gabby said. "But rumor had that it was about taxes. Sherm's the tax collector up this way as well as the sheriff, you know. In a community this small, we all wear several hats. Sherm can take a hard attitude when folks don't pay up right away. But Barbara being a widow, well, that made it hard for her to hold on to her land."

"How much land did she have?" Frank asked.

"Oh, quite a piece, a quarter of the island, or

even more," Gabby told them. In fact, it was Dexter's dad who first came up with the idea to form the special agreement to preserve the island. He was a good man. Loved the woods and loved the sea. But he died too young. Went out fishing one day, and never came back."

"Did Dexter's mother manage to hold on to her property?" Joe asked.

"There's something else I can't tell you for certain," the captain said. "Sherm is tight-lipped as can be about that kind of thing."

"There must be records," Joe said, his eyes brightening.

"Ayeh. They're in the town hall, I reckon. But it's closed for the day now. The government shuts down early on Makatunk," the captain explained. "Myra Johnson, the town clerk, likes to hang her laundry in the afternoons."

As they talked, the three had wandered farther out of town, along the path leading to Cathedral Forest. "We should check in on Chet pretty soon," Joe said, looking at the huge pine forest. "But let's take a minute here."

They stepped off the path and onto the soft carpet of pine needles in Cathedral Forest. "I've been coming here all my life," Gabby murmured, looking up at the trees with an expression of awe in his eyes. "There's nothing better on this earth, lads. Nothing."

Frank drank in a deep breath of the pure pine-scented air, and nodded appreciatively.

"It's so peaceful here," Joe said, his neck bent to the sky. "So still, so—"

But he never finished what he was about to say. For a sudden whooshing sound interrupted him, and the words stuck in his throat. An arrow was whizzing through the air. And it was headed straight for him!

9 Over the Cliffs

"Whoa!" Joe cried out, ducking instinctively. He felt a rush of air as the arrow flew by and embedded itself with a *thwunk* in the tall pine tree right behind him. "Who could be shooting at us?"

Frank and Gabby had crouched down, too. For a few moments the three of them stayed frozen, waiting to see if any other arrows would follow. The only sound they heard, though, was a bird crying in distress in a tree above them.

"Let's check out where that arrow came from," Frank said, cautiously standing up. "It must have been shot from the path leading into these woods." He darted through the trees, trying to keep out of view as much as possible.

"This is more than I bargained for when I came on this walk with you lads," Gabby said, looking around warily as he followed Frank and Joe out of the pines.

"Someone is out to get us," Joe told the captain."

The captain shot Joe a worried look and shook his head. "I knew something was wrong on the island, but I had no idea how serious it had become."

Out on the main trail there was nothing but wild roses and more forest. "I don't see anyone here," Frank said, running a hand through his dark hair and looking around.

Joe peered back at the open space in Cathedral Forest where he'd been standing when the arrow was shot. Gauging the path of the arrow, he turned and pushed through some bushes behind him. "Pay dirt!" he cried, reaching down to the ground. When he stood up, he was holding a bow and a quiver filled with arrows. "Look what someone left behind!"

Frank walked into the thicket and inspected the bow and quiver. They were professional hunting arrows and a strong, metal bow.

Gabby pushed through the bushes, bent down, and picked something up. "I wonder if this has anything to do with what happened," he said, and held out a small wooden object.

"What is that?" Frank asked, walking closer.

Gabby held up a lady's barrette.

"I've seen that hair clip before," Frank said, his eyes narrowing.

"In Nora Stricter's hair!" Joe finished for him.

"Nora Stricter? Shooting arrows? Trying to kill someone?" Gabby said, looking confused. "I've known Nora a goodly sum of years, boys. She's not the kind to be involved in something like this."

Joe took the barrette from Gabby's hand. "Maybe, and maybe not. Why else would her barrette be so near these arrows? You can never be sure, Gabby. People are not always what they seem."

"Ayeh. That's true enough," the captain said sadly. Then he stared at something behind Joe and Frank. "Well, here's your chance to ask her about it. Look there."

Frank spun around and saw Nora and two other Acorn Society members striding down the trail that started at the cliffs and led all the way to town.

The group silently approached, and without a word, Nora and her companions filed by. Frank's jaw fell open as they passed him. Each of them was carrying an arrow and the freckle-faced man was wearing an empty quiver! "Nora, wait!" Frank called.

The Acorn Society leader turned back to him with a cold look in her eyes. "Please don't shout," she admonished Frank. "You are upsetting the natural inhabitants."

Joe faced her squarely. "Maybe you'd like to explain why you or one of your pals here was trying to blast my head off!"

Nora shook her head slightly and gave Joe a pitying look. "I have no idea what you are talking

89

about, young man, but if you ran into trouble in Cathedral Forest, then you brought it on yourself. Apparently, you did not heed my warning. The lives of small animals may not seem important to you, my friend, but rest assured, there is justice in this world."

"What?" Joe said, scratching his head.

"True cosmic justice," she added.

"Nora," Gabby put in. "What's that got to do with the price of tea in China?"

"I distinctly warned these two about going into Cathedral Forest at this time of day," Nora said. "I told them it disturbs the feeding patterns of small wildlife there. I thought I had educated them, but apparently not. Some people refuse to learn."

"So that's why you fired an arrow at my brother's head?" Frank spoke up.

"Excuse me, I have not fired an arrow *at* anyone," Nora said.

"Oh, no?" Joe challenged. "Then how do you explain this?" He held the barrette up in front of her face.

"My barrette!" Nora said, surprised. "I lost it at the inn!" She quickly snatched the barrette from Joe's hand.

"Not so fast," Frank said, and gently pulled it out of her fingers. "We may need this as evidence."

Nora looked stunned. "What in the world are you talking about?"

"You know something," Joe said, steaming. "For a smart woman, you're kind of slow. We were talking about the arrow you shot at me, remember?"

"It does look kind of bad, Nora," Gabby put in. "I was with those fellas when the arrow shot by, and then we found this quiver and your barrette."

"That's not my quiver," Nora sniffed.

"Excuse me," said the freckle-faced man standing next to Nora. "I've been with Nora all day. She most definitely did not shoot any arrows at anyone or anything!"

Nora nodded in agreement. "Nonviolence toward all living things is one of the founding principles of the Acorn Society."

"Why do you have those arrows, then?" Frank asked.

"They're for ceremonial use," Nora explained. "Every year we climb down the cliffs by rope and toss our arrows into the ocean. Then we wait for the tide to return them to us. It's one of our Acorn Society rituals that helps focus our energies on the work we're trying to do."

"The idea behind it," the man explained, "is that our actions will come back to us."

"Then where is your bow!" Joe demanded. "We found the bow that had been used to fire at me hidden with the quiver."

Nora sighed and shook her head. "You just don't understand," she said in a condescending tone. "We break the arrows and throw them into the ocean as a symbol of commitment to nonaggression."

"Unfortunately, there were men with all sorts of equipment on the beach under the cliff today, and we weren't able to perform our ceremony," the other woman added.

Joe didn't look convinced.

"Look, Nora," Frank said. "A lot of dangerous things have been happening on Makatunk. Somebody is trying to get rid of most of the people on this island—the tourists, the artists, even the fishermen. We know you'd like to stop people from fishing here. So we figure you had a motive to cut a hole in Sherm Davis's boat."

"Someone did that? That's terrible!" Nora gasped. "Not that Sherm doesn't deserve it. He's a horrible person. He loves to go around telling people that I'm crazy. But he's the one who drags poor fish from their watery homes and sends them to untimely deaths, not me!"

Frank wondered if Nora knew about any of the other crimes that had taken place. Maybe she was working with someone, someone with a different set of grudges against the islanders. "There were also several paintings stolen from the Crawford Gallery," he began. "Kent Halliwell paintings."

Nora's reaction to that information surprised Frank. She seemed to be suppressing the urge to smile. "I take it you're not a Halliwell fan?" he asked her.

"Not at all," Nora said. "For all her wealth and fame, she's done nothing to help the wild creatures of this island. In fact, she's hurt them! Last fall, she razed a grove of beautiful old pines just so she could have a better view of the ocean."

"This arrow incident isn't the only dangerous run-in we've had," Joe said, jumping in. "Last night, the roof of the Webster Shack collapsed on us!"

Nora seemed genuinely concerned. "Do you think someone was purposely trying to harm you?" she asked.

"That's what we're trying to find out," Joe said, looking her right in the eye. "Someone sure tried to hurt the people at the inn by poisoning the fish. Any ideas about that, Nora?"

Immediately, Nora's expression returned to its customary glare.

"Young man," Nora shot back, "I have the distinct impression I'm being grilled. I'll have you know that I'm innocent, and if you insist on keeping up with these accusations, I'll have to consult a lawyer!" With that, she and her friends started back toward town.

"Whew," Gabby said, watching them go. "There's fire in that one."

"She certainly dislikes Kent Halliwell," Frank said. "That was new information."

"Well, lads, I've had enough excitement for one day," Gabby told them. "I'm going to head back home before my wife begins to wonder where I've wandered off to."

Frank and Joe thanked Gabby for his help and watched him go. "Frank," Joe said. "The woman with Nora just said that there were men on the beach under the cliff with equipment. I wonder if it was Glenn and Bob?"

"There's one way to find out," Frank said, turning onto the trail that led upward. "Let's go see."

"Did you notice that Glenn and Bob both ordered vegetarian platters last night?" Joe asked as they walked. "They don't exactly seem like vegetarians, either, especially since they first asked for steak and lamb chops. Maybe they had something to do with the salmonella poisoning?"

"The more we're on this case, the more I suspect they're involved," Frank said. "But how? And why? What's in it for them? And they weren't here when all these problems started back in the spring."

"Right," Joe said. "I forgot."

The brothers passed Kent Halliwell as they walked. The artist had a sketch pad under her arm, but only glared at them as she passed by. "She must have gotten the bad news about her paintings," Joe ventured after she'd tramped out of sight.

Soon the brothers came out onto the windy cliff. "There's no one down there, but I see some equipment on the beach," Frank said, peering over the edge. "Let's go check it out."

"Hey! Who left this rope here?" Joe said, surprised by the sight of two large coils sitting on the rocks on top of the cliff.

"I bet Nora and her group left them here. Remember, that woman said they weren't able to do their ceremony. They're probably planning to come back later," Frank said. "How lucky can we get? We can borrow them to rappel down the cliff face. It's not a totally sheer cliff, after all. We should be able to make it down pretty easily, and it'll save a lot of time if we don't have to go all the way around like last time."

"Great!" Joe said. He took a rope and tied it tightly around his waist. Frank did the same, then both boys tied the other ends of the ropes securely around a big tree near the edge of the cliff.

Soon the brothers were edging down the cliff face, grabbing handholds wherever they could find them. For the most part, there were plenty of places to get good footing. Finally, though, they came to a place where they were hanging over the edge of a precipice. "Boy, these ropes better hold," Frank said. "Once we get past here, it's clear sailing to the bottom."

Just as he said it, though, he felt his rope give way a little. "Hey!" he cried, his heart leaping to his throat. "What the—?"

At that moment, there was a twanging sound from above them, and Frank felt his rope give way altogether. "Joe!" he cried. "I'm falling!"

10 Blackout

"Frank, no!" Frank heard Joe screaming.

For a sickening moment, Frank felt himself free-falling. In that split-second, he reached out instinctively and grabbed the first thing he felt. It was rough and cut into his hand, but it was sturdy enough to break his fall.

Looking up, Frank saw that he had grabbed hold of a little tree that grew improbably out of a crevice on the cliff. He held on for dear life, hoping the little tree wouldn't break on him.

"Hold on, Frank!" Joe called out from above. "I'm coming. I'm—whoa!" Frank looked up, and saw Joe slip a foot or two. "My rope!" Joe cried.

"Someone's cutting it, like they cut mine!" Frank called back. "Hurry up and get a grip somewhere! Don't worry about me!"

"But you'll fall!" Joe shouted. "I can't let you—yaaah!" As another strand of Joe's rope was cut, he clung to the rock ledge next to him. From above, the rope came plummeting down at them. Joe had to duck to avoid being hit by it. He nearly lost his grip.

"Well, this is just great!" Joe said, breathing hard. "Now what do we do?"

Frank looked down. There was barely a toehold beneath him. Then he examined the tree he was hanging from. It couldn't have been more than four feet long from its roots to its crown. But the roots seemed incredibly strong. They wound in and out of the rocks, gripping them like octopus legs.

"See if you can swing your rope over here," Frank said. "I'll tie it around the roots of this tree, and then we can lower ourselves down."

"Are you kidding?" Joe asked. "That little tree will never hold the weight of both of us!"

"You got a better idea?" Frank asked. "Get moving! I can't hold on like this forever."

Joe grabbed hold of his rope, one end of which was tied around his waist. The tips of his shoes were barely holding on to a crevice in the rockface. He gathered the rope up into a coil with one hand, then threw it over to Frank.

Frank reached out his free hand and grabbed the rope on the first try. Then, hanging on with his other hand, he wound the rope around the trunk of the tree and some roots. He knotted it securely and then said, "Okay, Joe. Ready to swing loose?"

97

"You're sure about this?" Joe asked nervously.

"Nope," Frank said. "Come on, Tarzan. It's now or never."

"Okay," Joe said. He took a deep breath, and let go of the rock. The rope dropped him about twenty-five feet down, leaving him swinging just five feet above the rocks at the bottom of the cliff. The little tree shivered, but held.

"Now untie yourself!" Frank called. Joe did, and dropped the rest of the way, landing safely.

"Yahoo! It worked!" he called up to his brother. "Your turn, Frank, it's fun!"

"Do I have a choice?" Frank asked. He gathered up the rope and tied it securely around him. Then he pushed off from the tree, letting himself drop. The rope grabbed him just short of the bottom, and Joe was able to help him out of its grip, untying the knot as he held Frank up.

"Boy, how do you like that?" Joe asked when they were safe on solid ground. "Homemade bungee jumping!"

Frank laughed out of sheer relief. Then he looked up at the top of the cliff, which was partly hidden from view, and his expression grew serious. "The fact is, Joe, somebody cut our ropes. They didn't just both give way by themselves."

"Who knew we were out here?" Joe asked.

"Other than Gabby and Nora?" Frank asked. "Well, Kent Halliwell must have known."

"Nora could have doubled back and followed us," Joe said. "And what about Dexter? Where's he

98

been through all this? He knows this island like the back of his hand. He wouldn't even need a trail to follow us!"

"True," Frank acknowledged.

Joe was looking down at the sandy ground. "Someone's been taking photographs," he said.

Frank took a look around him. "I see a tidal pool full of starfish and anemones. But I don't see any photography equipment."

"Well, check this out," Joe said, pointing down to three marks in the sand. "These impressions had to have been made by a tripod. In fact, they're set up in the same position that our pals Glenn and Bob had them in last time. This is a great place to take pictures, but why would it be in the exact same place, facing the same direction?"

"And why would someone want so many pictures of a wall of rocks when the ocean is facing in the other direction?" Frank wondered aloud. "Well, one thing is sure. Salmonella or no salmonella, we're eating at the inn again tonight. I just can't get enough of Glenn and Bob's company, if you know what I mean."

"Amazing, bro," Joe said, patting Frank on the shoulder. "I feel exactly the same way."

The Hardys hurried back to Emma's to see how Chet was doing, and to fill him in on what had happened during the day. To their surprise, he had set up the easel on the porch and was standing behind it finishing a sketch of the town and water below.

"That's good, Chet," Joe said admiringly. "I didn't know you had any artistic ability."

"I didn't either," Chet said, clearly proud of his work. "I guess being on Makatunk inspired me."

Frank and Joe recounted the day's events. As they described their harrowing descent down the cliff, Chet sat down heavily in the wicker chair behind him. "Whew," he said, wiping his hand across his forehead. "I'm exhausted just listening to all this."

"Well, all this excitement has made me hungry." Joe said. "Are you guys ready to walk into town?"

"Actually, our neighbors, the Johnsons, invited me to have dinner at their house tonight," Chet said. "I didn't think you'd mind, so I said yes."

"Why should we mind?" Joe asked.

"The Johnsons," Frank repeated. "Chet, what's Mrs. Johnson's first name?"

"Myra."

"That's it! Myra Johnson!" Frank exclaimed. "She works in the town hall, right?"

"I think so," Chet replied.

"Gabby was telling us about her," Frank said. "Do you think she'd mind if we asked her a couple of questions?"

"Not at all," Chet said. "The Johnsons are both very friendly."

"Come on, then," Frank said, hopping off the porch and walking down the road to the house next door to Emma's, with Joe and Chet right behind him.

Myra Johnson answered Frank's knock with a

friendly, but flustered, hello. "Oh, my, you're early, Chet, and I didn't realize your friends would be coming."

"We won't be staying for dinner, Mrs. Johnson," Joe told her.

"Nonsense, I have plenty of food," she said with a pleasant smile. "I'll just put a couple of extra plates on the table."

"We have other plans," Frank explained. "But we're hoping you might be able to tell us a little something about Dexter Greenleaf and his family."

"Frank and Joe are trying to get to the bottom of the trouble on the island," Chet added.

"Today we heard that there were some problems with Dexter's mother paying land taxes," Frank told her. "Do you know anything about that?"

"How will knowing that help you get to the bottom of the problem?" Myra asked.

"I can't explain exactly how it will," he confessed, "but I know we're on the track of something."

"These guys are lucky to be alive!" Chet blurted out. "Whoever the culprit is seems to be mighty scared that Frank and Joe are about to blow the case wide open." He told Myra about some of the nearly fatal "accidents" Joe and Frank had recently experienced.

"So you see, whoever we're dealing with here is possibly very dangerous," Frank said. "That's why we're following every lead and hunch we get."

"Oh, my," Mrs. Johnson said, looking worried.

101

"I'm happy to tell you what I know, though I don't remember the figures exactly. Dexter owes quite a sum of money on his mother's property, I believe, and it comes due next month."

"How much land are we talking about?" Joe asked.

"I have a map right here and I can show you," Mrs. Johnson said. She walked over to a bookshelf and pulled out a large folded map.

"Let's see," she said, spreading the map open on the coffee table. "The Greenleaf property comes in two parcels. Here's the parcel that Dexter's house is on, and here's the Greenleaf land on the undeveloped side of the island, out by the cliffs."

Frank and Joe watched her finger outline a large triangle on the map. "Wow!" Joe said in amazement. "You mean, Dexter owns Cathedral Forest and the cliffs beyond it?"

"Technically speaking, yes," Mrs. Johnson said. "He has to pay taxes on it, even though it's part of the island land agreement and can never be developed."

"Who else owns the undeveloped part of the island?" Frank asked, curious.

"Oh, it's about equal between George Hubert and Sherm Davis," the town clerk told them. "A few other folks have small parcels, but nothing to speak of."

"Frank," Joe said, standing and pointing to a small clock on one of the end tables. "We've got to get to the inn. We want to be early, remember?"

"Just one more question, Mrs. Johnson," Frank said, rising. "What happens if Dexter can't pay?"

"Why then the property goes up for auction for back taxes," she explained. "That's a cheap way of acquiring property in most places. But because of the agreement, whoever bought that land wouldn't be able to build on it. Not many people care to buy land that can't be developed."

"I see," Frank said thoughtfully as he made his way to the door.

"I hope I've been of some use to you," Mrs. Johnson said at the door.

"You've been extremely helpful, thanks," Frank said. "Good night. See you later, Chet."

Frank and Joe were soon hurrying down the road to the inn. "Now we know why Dexter works so hard, at least," Joe said.

"Yes, but it's kind of strange to think of Dexter as a major land owner, isn't it?" Frank replied. "He certainly doesn't act the part."

"Sounds like he's barely holding on to the property." Joe stuck his hands in his pockets, thinking.

They reached the inn shortly before it was time for the dinner bell. Brian was in the lobby, checking the guest registry. He wasn't wearing his usual Makatunk Inn T-shirt. "Hi," Frank said with a wave. Brian looked up and smiled a greeting.

"Aren't you working in the dining room tonight?" Joe asked.

"I found this note for Mr. Carter, and I was going

to bring it up to his room before I changed," Brian explained.

"Where did you find it?" Frank asked.

"That's the strange part," Brian said. "It was in the dining room, propped up on a table when I first went in to fold napkins."

"We're on our way up to Glenn's room now," Joe said cheerfully. "We'll give it to him for you."

"Great," Brian said, handing Joe the note. "I'm running late!"

As soon as they got to the stair landing, where no one could see them, Joe opened the envelope. "We're lucky," he said. "The damp air kept this envelope from sealing properly." Eagerly the boys scanned the typewritten note: THE HARDY BROTHERS ARE MAKING MY LIFE VERY DIFFICULT. MEET ME IN THE MEADOW BEHIND THE TOWN HALL AT 10 P.M. AND BRING BOB.

Frank met Joe's eyes and grinned.

"Finally!" Frank said, excited. "A real break in the case."

Joe nodded in agreement. "I know where we'll be tonight," he said.

"Not so fast, Joe," Frank advised. "I have a better idea. Why don't I go to the meadow alone? That way you can take another look in their rooms. They're bound to be out of the way for a while. I can head back and warn you when they're on their way back."

"Good thinking," Joe said approvingly. He

resealed the envelope as best he could and shoved it under Glenn Carter's door.

"Let's go!" Joe whispered. He darted down the hall, with Frank right behind him.

In the dining room, Frank and Joe sat down at the same table as Glenn and Bob. But the Hardys weren't able to draw much out of the two men. Frank started a conversation about photography, but he didn't get very far. For two guys who were taking a tripod to the cliffs every day, they didn't seem to know much, or care much, about photography.

The men ate quickly and excused themselves at about seven forty-five. "See you at the meadow, guys," Frank murmured under his breath, as he watched them go. Joe smiled.

The Hardy brothers spent the evening with the teenage staff of the inn, mostly tossing a Frisbee on the lawn while the sun went down. The game broke up at dark, when most of the staff turned in. Frank and Joe sat on the porch, waiting for ten o'clock.

"We may actually have this whole case solved tonight," Joe said excitedly, "once we find out who they're meeting and what they all have to say."

"Well, I promise to tell you all about it," Frank said with a grin. "And I can't wait to hear about what you find in their rooms."

"As soon as I get a good look around, I'll come rescue you," Joe said.

"You mean, you'll join me," Frank corrected him. "I'm not planning to need a rescue!"

"Shhh! Here they come!" Joe said.

The boys retreated to the corner of the wrap-around porch as Glenn and Bob stepped out of the hotel and went off down the road. Joe patted Frank on the back, and headed inside. Frank slipped off into the darkness, keeping a safe distance behind the two men.

At the corner of Robinson Road, Glenn and Bob headed around the municipal building to the meadow in back. Frank heard the foghorn sound from the top of the hill. Clouds were blotting out the stars, and except for the beams of the lighthouse and Glenn and Bob's flashlight it was totally dark.

Suddenly, Frank heard a rustling noise behind him. He froze, just about to wheel around, when a strong hand covered his mouth, pressing a handkerchief to it.

Frank inhaled a sickly sweet smell. He tried to struggle, but the next thing he knew, everything went black!

11 A Warning

Joe Hardy climbed the stairs and crept down the hallway to the door of room 227. From behind the doors of the various rooms he passed, he could hear the sounds of conversation, a shower, and even someone snoring. Joe realized that on a quiet island like Makatunk, people turned in just after dark, and got up with the sunrise.

As he pulled his trusty Swiss Army knife out of his pocket and opened it, he looked over his shoulder to make sure no one was coming. Then he inserted the open blade into the old lock and jiggled it.

The door opened quickly, and Joe slipped inside the dark room. He pulled his penlight out of his pocket, flicked it on, and looked around the room. He spied the laptop computer and opened it, hoping to find a clue. But he was stopped at once when the computer asked for a password he didn't know.

Joe tried the ledger book next, but it held no clues other than the ones Frank had already seen.

The tripod that he and Frank had seen at the cliff was standing in the corner, the camera still on it. But on closer inspection, Joe saw that it wasn't a camera at all. It was the kind of scope used for land surveying! Now, why were Glenn Carter and Bob D'Amico spending their vacation surveying land? he wondered. It didn't make sense.

Penlight in hand, Joe dropped to his knees and peered under the bed. What he saw there piqued his interest quite a bit. He saw a large, rolled-up scroll—not the kind of thing people usually bring on vacation.

Joe put the scroll on the bed and unrolled it, holding the ends down with two books. Then he aimed his small beam of light at the large paper. The very title on the top of the scroll caused him to let out a low whistle. It read: THE MAKATUNK ISLAND SUPER-RESORT—STAGE-ONE PROJECTION.

The scroll was actually a map of Makatunk Island. But it wasn't the Makatunk Island Joe had come to know. Nor was it like the hand-drawn map he and Frank carried, or even the one he'd just seen at Myra Johnson's. This map showed a Makatunk Island that didn't exist—at least not yet.

His heart hammering wildly, Joe studied the map, knowing he'd found an important clue. It was a sophisticated, three-dimensional, computer-generated topographical map. On it, Makatunk Island had a huge marina centered around the old shipwreck, dozens of tennis courts, and a huge heated saltwater pool where the meadow should have been. Instead of the Makatunk Inn, there was a twelve-story hexagonal hotel, shaped like a lighthouse. The tall hotel had a rotating restaurant on top, named the Lobster Palace.

On the other end of the island was a championship golf course that wound through Cathedral Forest and out onto the cliffs. "That's why they were surveying that day!" Joe said aloud, looking at the golf course's fourteenth green, which lay next to the tidal pool, protected from the surf by a modern-looking sea wall.

Then Joe's eyes focused on the words on the bottom of the scroll. "Resorts Horizons Industries," he read aloud. "RHI. That's it!" He gasped.

Taking one last look at the map, Joe's thoughts raced, trying to put all the pieces together. Obviously, Resorts Horizons Industries planned to take over the island. All of the vandalism, all of the problems were RHI's attempts to get most of the locals out of the way.

But, Joe remembered, Glenn and Bob had only just arrived on the island, and the trouble had started back in the spring. And how could the corporation get around the land agreement that preserved the natural state of a large portion of the island?

A shudder made its way down Joe's spine as a

hard, ugly truth hit him. There had to be an insider on Makatunk Island who was working for the corporation—someone who was willing to sell the place out. Someone who would do whatever was necessary to get the job done. Sabotaging Sherm's boat, poisoning the dinner at the inn, causing the collapse of the shack, cutting the ropes on the cliff—these were all the acts of someone willing to go as far as murder!

Joe didn't waste another moment. He rolled up the scroll and took it with him to show to Frank, and then to Sherm when he got back from the mainland in the morning.

Excited by the new break in the case, he hurried out of the room, not bothering to put anything back in its place. With the scroll missing, Glenn and Bob would know someone had been there—in fact, they'd probably know who it was.

Joe crept downstairs and out of the inn. The air was chillier than usual, and a wind was coming from the east. Joe picked up his collar against the wind and hurried along the darkened road. He couldn't wait to get to Frank and tell him what he'd learned.

Perhaps Frank would have even more evidence! That note they'd intercepted had probably been from the island accomplice. That must have been who Glenn and Bob were meeting. With any luck, Frank would have the missing piece of the puzzle: The identity of the insider who was working with the corporation.

Just as he rounded the small municipal building,

Joe saw the large, dark shape of something lying in the road. "Frank!" He gasped as he got closer. Frank was lying on the ground, unconscious. "Frank, are you okay?" Joe quickly found Frank's pulse, and was relieved to discover it was normal. Then he propped his brother up and very lightly slapped his cheeks.

"Ooohhh," Frank moaned, coming to. Joe smelled something sweet on the skin of Frank's face. "Somebody . . . chloroformed me," Frank said, panting. "I don't know who, though."

Joe helped Frank up, and the two made their way slowly up the hill, while Joe told Frank what he'd found. A sharp breeze followed them and Frank started shivering. When they arrived at the house, Joe bounded upstairs, and found Chet in his bedroom reading by the light of a kerosene lamp.

"Wait till you see this, Chet," Joe cried, rushing into the room with the scroll under his arm. Frank followed a close step behind.

Chet looked from Joe to Frank, confused. "Joe looks thrilled," he said. "But you look terrible, Frank. What's going on?"

"I was chloroformed, that's all," Frank said, sitting on the edge of Chet's bed. "But that's not important. Listen to what Joe found out."

When Joe set the map out, Chet's eyes grew wide. "This is totally disgusting!" he cried.

"Just one thing, Joe," Frank said. "How are Glenn and Bob going to take the fact that we've got their map? I don't think they'll be too pleased."

111

Joe scratched his head. "I see what you're thinking," he murmured. "You're afraid they might come after us tonight."

"Or set their accomplice on you, whoever that is!" Chet said, sitting up with a jolt. "I don't know about this, guys."

"Tomorrow we'll go see Sherm as soon as he gets back," Frank said.

"We'd better lock up good tonight," Chet said with a shiver. "I wish Aunt Emma had a deadbolt or a police lock or something."

"I'll go put chairs in front of the doors," Joe suggested, walking to the door of Chet's bedroom, with Frank behind him.

But the Hardys froze in their tracks when they heard the front door suddenly swing open downstairs. A gust of wind swept all the way up the darkened stairway, and with it came a deep booming voice. "I hope you're prepared!" the voice warned. "'Cause tonight's a good night to die!"

12 Dexter's Secret

For a moment, the three boys stood frozen at the top of the landing. Uncertain of the best course of action, they exchanged quick glances, their eyes wide.

Well, dying is not in our plans for tonight, Joe thought to himself as he crept closer to the top of the stairs. Steeling himself, he craned his neck and looked down.

There, in the middle of the living room, stood a portly man with red hair. He held an old-fashioned outdoor oil lamp in his outstretched arm. "Boys," he called. "Are you at home?"

"Mr. Johnson!" Chet said, walking around Joe and Frank and going downstairs. "You practically scared us to death!"

"I just touched the door and it flew open! That's how bad the wind has gotten," the man explained. "But I had to come over and tell you, there's a dangerous storm rising. A big one. Myra and I just heard about it on our battery-powered radio. You'll be wanting to lock and shutter all your windows tonight, or there'll be glass all over the place by morning."

"Thanks for the warning," Frank said, walking downstairs to shut the door as Mr. Johnson left.

"Actually, we were planning on locking them anyway," Joe said with a tight grin, looking over in Frank and Chet's direction. "Well, guys, time for beddy-bye. Sleep well, Chet."

"Oh, I'm sure I'll sleep just like a baby," Chet said sarcastically. "I'll wake up every two hours and cry!"

The next morning, the first thing Frank noticed was the chill in the house and the rain hitting the window. "Time's wasting," he called to Joe, who was buried chin first in his pillow.

By eight o'clock, though, both Hardys were dressed. Chet had done some shopping the day before and after a quick breakfast of fruit, cold cereal, and milk, the Hardys were ready to head down to Sherm Davis's house. The *Maine Maiden* was arriving, as they could see looking out the picture window in the living room.

Chet was going to stay at Emma's house to guard the map which was carefully hidden behind the headboard of Chet's bed. Chet locked the door behind Frank and Joe, and gave them a thumbs-up sign through the glass.

The wind and rain whipped around the Hardys. "It's a good thing that we brought rain ponchos with us," Joe said as a gust of wind nearly blew him sideways.

"Yep," Frank agreed. "Getting soaked on the boat was enough for me."

They hurried to the sheriff's house. "Come on in, boys," he said when they knocked on the door. "I just got home and I'm making my morning cup of coffee."

The boys shook the water off their ponchos before going inside.

"Sherm, a lot happened last night," Frank said, following him into his small blue and white kitchen.

The brothers told the sheriff everything as Sherm puttered around the kitchen, listening intently, with a grim look on his face.

"You should bring that map over here for me to hold," he said. "Otherwise those two fellas are liable to come after you to get it back."

"No, thanks. Last time we left something here, it got stolen, remember?" Frank said, referring to the vial of salmonella.

"True, true," Sherm said sheepishly. "Well, take good care of it. It might be evidence."

"What are you planning to do about Glenn and Bob?" Joe blurted out.

"What can I do?" Sherm asked. "I can't arrest

them. They haven't broken any laws, as far as I can tell."

"Sherm, what did they tell you on the mainland yesterday?" Frank asked, hoping to find some clear, decisive direction to follow in this case.

Instead, he got the opposite. "When I talked it over with my superiors, they suggested I take the investigation slower," Sherm answered. "They think I'm rushing things."

"Rushing?" Joe said in disbelief. "Do they have any idea how dangerous the situation is?"

"Did you tell them there have been attempts on people's lives?" Frank added.

"I sure did," Sherm told them as he poured milk in his coffee. "Told them things were real bad around here. And they told me I was overreacting."

"What did they say when you told them about the salmonella poisoning?" Joe asked.

"They said they get salmonella cases all the time on the mainland. They said it might have come from conditions in the kitchen or that the food poisoning could have been coincidental. That vial was never tested, you know. It might not have had poison in it at all. Might have been a prank! Even if it was salmonella, like the doctor thought, who are we going to nab for it?" Sherm said with a shrug.

Frank didn't like what he was hearing. "Sherm, do us a favor, will you?" he pleaded. "Let us talk to the police on the mainland. Maybe we could communicate what's going on here with a little more urgency than you can."

116

"I'd love to have you do that," Sherm said, picking up the cup. "Trouble is, with the storm, this island is *incommunicado*."

"What does that mean?" Joe demanded.

"Very simply," the sheriff told him. "We can't reach the mainland police until the weather clears."

"Sherm," Frank said, leveling with him. "Is it true that Dexter was sent to a detention center for threatening you with a deadly weapon?"

Sherm frowned. "Well, now you see why I didn't want to mention it. After all, that incident happened a long time ago," the sheriff said. "Dexter has a right to try to make a new life for himself. If he's capable of it, that is."

"We were also told that his mother had a large piece of property—" Joe added.

The sheriff stood up so suddenly, his coffee nearly sloshed out of the cup. "Here I sit, and I forgot to get the small-craft warning out! I've got to get back to the dock to warn folks away from the water or we may lose some lives!" He got up and raced to the kitchen door, grabbing a yellow slicker from a hook as he went. "I'll tell you about the Greenleaf land later. With this storm coming on, I'll have a lot to do. This is an emergency!"

With that, the sheriff was gone. The brothers were silent for a moment as they watched him hurry through his backyard.

"That was weird," Joe said, as rain pelted against the kitchen window.

117

"Very," Frank agreed. "But I guess we should reserve judgment about it for the moment. After all, this is pretty severe weather."

"Where to now? Dexter's?" Joe asked.

"Great minds think alike," Frank said. "I was just going to suggest that. He lives pretty close by. Myra Johnson pointed to his place on the map last night, remember?"

Frank and Joe left Sherm's house and took off onto a trail that passed Dexter's place. By the time they got there, their shoes were soaked.

"Dexter? Dexter!" Frank shouted, knocking on the door of the modest frame shanty. Even in the rain, he noticed a fairly large vegetable garden next to Dexter's house. Dexter didn't seem like the type to garden, but, then, he didn't seem like a major land owner either.

"I guess he's not around," Joe said, after they'd knocked for several minutes with no response. "Should we go look for him?"

Frank was about to answer, when he heard the sound of a truck approaching. "Here he comes now!" he said. "Let's hide and see what he does."

The two boys ducked behind the woodpile in Dexter's yard, and watched him drive up in his truck. Dexter got out and looked around cautiously, as if he wanted to make sure no one was watching. Then he went to the back of his truck, which had two big boxes on it, each covered with a large tarpaulin.

Dexter peeked under the tarpaulin, then looked

around nervously again. "I wonder what he's got under there," Joe whispered to Frank. "Stolen goods, maybe?"

"Maybe," Frank whispered back.

Dexter grabbed one of the boxes, which the boys thought must have been quite heavy, judging by the way he grunted under the load. He put it down for a moment to unlock his front door, brought the box inside, and then came back out for the other one. When he had brought that one inside, Frank motioned Joe to follow him, and the boys crept up to one of the front windows. There, they watched as Dexter took the tarpaulins off the boxes.

"I can't believe it!" Joe gasped as he saw what was in them.

Frank let out a low whistle. "He's got Kent Halliwell's dogs!"

13 Chet's Disappearance

Frank and Joe both looked toward the door, which they realized was still unlocked. "Now!" Frank whispered. "Before he has a chance to let the dogs loose on us!"

In an instant, the boys sprang for the door. Frank twisted the knob, and Joe burst through, yelling, "Freeze, Dexter! We've caught you red-handed this time!"

Dexter shouted in surprise and spun around. In sheer panic, he reached for the latch of one of the dogs' cages. But Frank lashed out with a karate kick that hit Dexter square in the wrist. Dexter pulled back his hand with a yowl of pain, just as Joe jumped on his back.

Moments later, the brothers had subdued the big islander. "All right! All right, I confess!" Dexter shouted, as Joe held his arms tightly behind his back.

"Aha!" Joe said triumphantly, and strengthened his grip.

"Tell us all about it, Dexter," Frank said, jumping in, as the dogs growled menacingly.

"Halliwell was mistreating them," Dexter explained miserably, looking at the dogs. "Didn't feed them half the time, just to keep them mean. And she hit them, too. I saw her! No wonder they're killers. I couldn't stand it. That's why I took them."

Frank and Joe looked at each other, startled. "What about all the other stuff?" Joe asked. "That arrow you fired at me, the rope you cut out at the cliff, the beam that fell on our heads—"

"The salmonella outbreak at the inn," Frank added.

"Huh?" Dexter grunted, confused. "What are you talking about? I didn't do any of those things! Did Sherm say I did? If he did, he's lying!"

"Sherm didn't tell us a thing," Joe said. "In fact, he told us he promised your mother not to talk to anyone about your past problems."

"What a phony!" Dexter spat out. "You want to hear the truth? I'll give it to you! After my dad died, Sherm started coming around pretending he wanted to help my ma. He made a big show of offering to relieve her of what he called our 'worthless parcel' of land. He kept saying how it was too bad she was stuck with it and that she could never build on it, and that it would just keep costing her

121

more and more each year. He told her he'd let her stay in this house rent-free if she'd sign the land over to him. He got her to sign a paper about it, too!

"As soon as she'd done it she regretted it. Well, when I found out about it, I borrowed a rifle and went over and got that paper back. I told Sherm I'd blast him on the spot if he didn't tear it up. My pa loved that land, and I hated to see it out of the family. Maybe I was wrong to go after him that way, but he was wrong, too. He took advantage of my ma, when she was so sad and worried about everything. He knew it, too."

"Is that how you ended up at the detention center?" Frank questioned.

"How'd you know about that?" Dexter asked, startled. When Frank and Joe didn't answer, Dexter shook his head and then continued.

"Yeah, Sherm got me sent away. But at least he didn't get the land, and my mother finally saw him for what he was. Mr. Hubert helped her out with a loan so she could keep our property. I'm still paying it back. Now I'm trying to put together enough money to make sure I don't lose the land to taxes."

"So you're saying you aren't responsible for any of the crimes that have taken place on Makatunk Island?" Joe asked in disbelief.

"Of course not!" Dexter said, indignantly. "Why would I? All I did was steal these two dogs. Okay, and those two cats over there in the corner. Old Farley was kicking them around too much, and he never missed them anyway. I like animals, see, and I can't stand to see them treated bad. They're nicer than most people," he grumbled, craning his neck to look around at Joe. Joe finally relaxed his grip on Dexter, who immediately went over to the dogs and began murmuring to them in a soothing tone, trying to get them to calm down.

Frank watched Dexter and then looked over at the two cats in the corner. They were obviously well cared for and well-fed, even though they were staring very cautiously at the Dobermans in the cages. Frank exchanged a glance with Joe, who seemed just as confused as he was.

Could Dexter really be innocent of all the crimes? Frank wondered. Or was he trying to bluff them with his sad story about his mother being pressured by Sherm? Sherm was the island tax collector after all. He had an obligation to collect taxes, no matter what people's individual circumstances were.

"Dexter, what do you know about those two businessmen who are staying at the inn?" Frank asked, trying another approach. "You know, the ones who wear ties with their hiking gear."

Dexter turned from the row of placid Dobermans.

"Ayeh, I seen them," Dexter said. "What about them?"

"We think they're behind everything that's going on," Joe explained. "We think they're working with an islander, too. Frankly, we thought it might be you."

"Ha!" Dexter laughed out loud. "I can't stand city folks. Why would I be working with them?"

"Money," Frank answered coolly. "You just told us how much you need it. Well, they want to build a resort here on the island, and they must be offering good money to anyone who'll help them drive everybody else out."

"How'd you find out so much?" Dexter asked.

"Our friend Chet loves this island," Joe said. "We offered to help get to the bottom of things, that's all." Joe didn't think he should let Dexter know that he and Frank were detectives. Despite this surprising new side of Dexter's, he still was a suspect.

"Well, if you are getting information from Sherm Davis you can forget about my help," Dexter said frowning. "That man's my enemy. And he's got you two wasting your time running around after me. Ha!"

"Listen, Dexter," Frank said. "You know you've got to return these pets to their owners."

"I will," Dexter said with a sigh. "I'll just let them have a little vacation. I'll give them back in a day or so. Maybe then their owners will appreciate them more and take better care of them, you know, if they missed them a little."

"Come on, Joe. Let's get out of here," Frank said, leading his brother back out into the rain.

"Can you beat that?" Joe asked when they were outside. "I actually felt sorry for the guy."

124

"Me, too," Frank said, surprised to find that he agreed. "Did you believe him?"

"He was pretty convincing," Joe said. "Still, he might be more clever than he seems, throwing a hard-luck story on us just to get our sympathies."

"If what he said was true, it sure gives him a strong motive to put a hole in Sherm's boat, though," Frank reasoned out loud.

"Frank, I think I'd better stay here and keep an eye on him," Joe offered. "Why don't you go down and talk to Mr. Hubert?"

"It's the truth," Mr. Hubert told Frank, as they sat in front of the huge fire blazing in the inn's fireplace. Outside, the winds were howling, and the sea was raging as rain splashed down everywhere. "Barbara Greenleaf sat right where you're sitting now and told me she signed everything over to Sherm, in exchange for his paying the taxes on her land. She said he pressured her something awful, and I believed her, because I saw how he went after my holdings!"

Frank was taken aback by Hubert's words. "Sherm wanted to buy the inn?" he asked.

"Oh, he's been after it for some time now," Hubert said. "Especially over the past few months. To tell the truth, lately I've been thinking of taking him up on his offer, too, what with business down the way it is."

"Mr. Hubert, do you know anything about a

company called RHI? Resorts Horizons Industries?" Frank asked suddenly.

It was a long shot, but it paid off. Hubert's eyebrows shot up, and he nodded. "I sure do," he said. "How do you know about them?"

"Never mind that," Frank said. "What do you know about the company?"

"They sent a young lady out to the island last summer offering to buy me out. Not bad money, but I would never sell the place to outsiders. Especially not some big company that might ruin the place altogether."

"I'm afraid that's exactly what they're planning to do," Frank told him. "Thank you, Mr. Hubert. You've been very cooperative. I think we may be close to nailing down this case."

Leaving the inn, Frank hurried back to Emma's house in the pouring rain and gusting wind. He planned to check in on Chet, and then go get Joe. The time had come for a long talk with the sheriff.

"Chet!" he called, banging on the locked door. There was no answer.

He fished for the key from his pocket, then cautiously opened the door and entered the house. It was eerily quiet inside. After calling Chet's name again, Frank raced up the stairs, taking them two at a time. But Chet was nowhere to be found.

Something was wrong, very wrong. Frank was sure of that as he went back downstairs. Why would Chet go out in the gathering storm if he didn't have to? Scanning the living room, Frank spotted a note on the coffee table. Momentarily relieved, he went over and picked it up.

" 'Dear Frank and Joe,' " he read aloud. " 'Those two RHI guys were here snooping around this morning, asking for you. They asked if I'd seen the map. I said no, but I don't think they believed me. They just left, but I don't trust them, so I'm going to follow them. P.S. Don't worry, I'm taking the map with me. Chet.' "

Frank's heart sank as he quickly folded the note and stuck it in his pocket. These guys were dangerous. Didn't Chet realize that if he made even the tiniest slipup, he could wind up paying with his life?

14 The Accomplice

Frank shot out of Emma's house like a cannonball. There wasn't a second to lose. If he and Joe, with all their detective skills, had nearly been killed several times on this case, what were Chet's chances?

On Hawk's Hill Road, he saw Nora and the Acorn Society members coming down from the direction of the cliffs. They seemed totally unfazed by the worsening storm, with its winds whipping up now in mighty gusts.

"Excuse me!" Frank called out, running to them, "I'm looking for Chet. You know, the husky guy?"

Nora blinked her eyes and glared at him from under the hood of her slicker. "Haven't I already told you about shouting? And I am tired of answering your questions, young man!"

"Please, this is important. Did you see anyone on your way back from the cliff?" Frank asked.

"Of course not," Nora said, "No one goes out on a day like today. In our society, people fear storms, because they fear nature. We in the Acorn Society are comfortable with all the expressions of the glory that is—"

"Nora, please!" Frank broke in. "This is an emergency! My friend is missing."

"Maybe we could help look for your friend," the man next to Nora suggested. "Compassion for our fellow human beings is also a founding principle of the Acorn Society."

"I'd really appreciate it," Frank said gratefully. "I have reason to believe that the criminals who have been vandalizing the island may be after him. He has something they want."

"What is that?" a woman in the group asked.

"I don't have time to explain. I've got to go get my brother," Frank told them.

"We'll fan out and search the area, and if we find Chet, we'll bring him to the inn," Nora said.

"Thanks very much, Nora," Frank said. "I really appreciate your help."

Nora nodded and turned to the stragglers in her group, who were just coming down from the cliff area. "We're calling a halt to our storm walk so we can help search for a missing person."

I'm glad Nora cares about people as much as she cares about nature, Frank thought, as he raced down to Dexter's place. By the time he got there, he was soaked to the bone and out of breath. He found Joe standing in Dexter's yard, hidden from the house by some bushes. "Chet's gone!" Frank told his brother. He pulled Chet's note from his pocket and handed it to Joe.

"Chet, bad move!" Joe cried in frustration.

"He didn't go up Hawk's Hill Road, so maybe he went down the main road. Let's try it," Frank suggested.

By the time they reached the main road, the rain was steady, and day had grown almost as dark as night. The wind still howled, sending the surf crashing against the rocks, even in the shelter of the harbor. Boats rocked on the waves like toys in a bathtub. In the distance, over the mainland, streaks of lightning were flashing everywhere.

The Hardys passed the volunteer fire station, where the islanders were getting the pump wagon ready. It was a small vehicle that held water to put out fires.

"Have you fellas seen Dexter?" asked Edgar, one of the men they'd seen fighting on the dock that first day on Makatunk. "He'd better get down here with that truck of his. If lightning starts a fire, we've got to stop it before it spreads!"

"Where's our sheriff, that's what I'd like to know!" added Farley, the fisherman who had had his traps stolen. "He's supposed to be a public official, but now that the public needs him, he's disappeared!"

130

"Sherm was on his way to the dock a while ago," Frank said.

"Well, he ain't there now," Farley replied. "I just went down to see."

Looking at the tiny pump wagon, Frank didn't think there would be much chance of keeping a fire from spreading. He asked the volunteers if they'd seen Chet, Glenn, or Bob, but they said they hadn't.

Joe and Frank continued through town, past the art gallery and the coffee shop. Both were boarded up tight. In fact, all through town, wooden shutters had been closed against the storm.

"Everyone says this is such a small island, but when you're looking for somebody, it gets a whole lot bigger," Joe complained.

"You can say that again," Frank said with a sigh. "Chet could be inside any building on the island, and even with all the people we've got searching, no one would see him."

"If only there was a way to contact the police on the mainland," Joe said. "They'd get out here, storm or no storm, and they'd bring police dogs with them to find Chet, and—"

"It's no use, Joe," Frank said. "We both know all the phones on the island are out. There's no way to get in touch with the mainland."

"Did I hear you boys say you wanted to contact the mainland?" a voice behind them asked. Turning, Frank saw that it was Mr. Hubert, wearing a Mackinaw and a waterproof rain hat. "I was just down to the wharf, to check on my boat and make sure she was battened down tight. It's going to be a bad one."

"Yes. Our friend Chet is missing, and we think he may be in danger," Frank said. "He was following Glenn Carter and Bob D'Amico, the guys who work for RHI!"

Mr. Hubert blinked twice and frowned. "Well, if you want to contact the mainland, why don't you use Sherm's ham radio?"

Frank and Joe looked at him, stunned. "Sherm's got a radio?" Joe gasped.

"Sure he does," Mr. Hubert said. "He's the sheriff, ain't he? Sheriff's got to have one, just in case of emergencies."

"Why didn't he mention it before?" Frank asked.

"Because he's a phony and a liar, just like Dexter said!" Joe said, suddenly exploding. "It's so clear to me now, Frank. Sherm Davis is the insider we're looking for!" Joe knocked his palm up against his forehead. "How could we have missed it?"

"I think I know how," Frank said, steaming, "Because of that hole in his boat."

"He took us out on that little pleasure jaunt just to throw us off track, right from the start!" Joe said, steaming mad.

"But we still need proof, Joe," Frank stressed. "Remember what Dad says. It doesn't matter if we think he's guilty, no court will buy it unless we get proof." Fenton Hardy, the boys' father, was a high-ranking police detective back in Bayport. His

132

long years of experience had taught him a lot, and he'd passed on his knowledge to his sons.

"You boys have lost me, I'm afraid," Mr. Hubert said, looking from one brother to the other.

"No time to explain," Frank told him. "We've got to get to that radio."

Sherm's house wasn't far from where they were. They hurried over to it, forced the door open, and went inside. "Sherm's not going to like this one bit," Hubert said happily. "Transmitter's probably upstairs, in his office."

"I thought his office was down here," Frank said.

"No," Hubert said. "That's his storeroom."

They all rushed upstairs to the office. Sitting on the table was the radio setup. Frank quickly sat down in front of it and began fiddling with the dials. Joe stood beside him, holding the headset to his ear.

"Nothing!" Joe grumbled. "Why aren't you getting a frequency?"

"I think this may be why," Mr. Hubert said from the other side of the table. The boys leaned over to see what he was pointing at.

"The wire that connects to the battery is gone!" Frank said grimly.

"Let's fix it!" Joe urged.

"We don't have time to try to track down another wire," Frank said. "Not with Chet still missing."

"Rats!" Joe exclaimed, kicking over a metal wastebasket by the table in his frustration.

"Sherm wasn't taking any chances," Frank said. "He must have removed the wire just in case we found this."

"Hey, what's this?" Joe suddenly said, bending down. Joe picked up a strongbox from under the desk near the basket he'd kicked. Sticking out of the strongbox was the corner of a hundred-dollar bill.

"Let's see that," Frank said, excited. The box was locked, but Frank flicked open his pocketknife and jimmied the lock. He raised the lid, and gasped in surprise. Inside the box were stacks and stacks of hundred-dollar bills!

"Where did Sherm get this kind of money?" Mr. Hubert said, fingering the bills. "There must be fifty thousand in here at least!"

Under the cash was a piece of stationery with RHI on the letterhead. Frank picked it up and read it aloud. " 'Owed by RHI—additional twelve thousand five hundred. Due August fifteenth.' " Frank pocketed the note and turned to the others. "Joe, you genius!" he said jubilantly. "You just stumbled upon our proof!"

15 At the Ice House

"Are you boys saying what I think you're saying?" Mr. Hubert asked, staring down at the stacks of bills Joe had discovered.

Frank spelled it out for him. "Sherm Davis has been working with Resorts Horizons Industries to destroy Makatunk Island."

"He probably broke his own lock just to make it look like somebody else took that salmonella bacteria," Joe added.

"To think," Frank said, shaking his head, "that I put that poison right in his hands!"

"I guess he was the perfect one for the corporation to approach. Who has more power and knows more about the island than the sheriff?" Joe asked in disgust.

"Hey!" Frank said suddenly. "While we're here

135

talking, Chet's still missing. We can figure this all out later. There isn't a moment to lose!"

"How can I help?" Mr. Hubert asked.

"Go tell everyone you meet to keep an eye out for Sherm as well as Chet and the two guys," Frank told him. "And when they see Sherm, to stick with him so he can't do any more damage!"

"I'm off," Mr. Hubert said. "Good luck, boys. I always knew that Sherm was a bad one. Now maybe we'll be rid of him."

The boys went outside after Mr. Hubert left. The rain had lost some of its intensity and the wind had lessened, but the sound of distant thunder signaled that the storm was far from over.

"Now where could Chet have gone?" Joe asked, looking around at the village and the wharf.

"Think for a minute, Joe," Frank said. "If you were Glenn and Bob, and you figured that the map was at our place, what would you do?"

"Double back and steal it," Joe said.

"But they couldn't because Chet was there," Frank pointed out.

"Well, then I'd go to see Sherm, to see if he had any ideas about how to get the map back," Joe suggested.

"My thoughts exactly!" Frank said. "They would have come here first, with Chet following right behind them. And then what?" Frank scratched his head, looking around him.

"Wherever they took him, they must have started out from this house," Joe said.

"Except that if they came out the front door, people might see them," Frank pointed out. "So maybe they went out the back door."

Quickly, the boys ran around to the back of the house. The backyard was sheltered by tall birch trees, and there was a path leading into the woods.

"What's that?" Frank said, pointing to the ground on the path.

"This stuff looks like a piece of a soaked chocolate chip cookie," Joe said, kneeling down and examining it more closely. "That's what it is! And there's another one, and another leading this way!"

"Good old Chet!" Frank said with a little laugh. "He may be reckless, but at least he remembered his 'Hansel and Gretel.'"

"Come on, let's go after him!" Joe cried.

The boys hurried down the path into the woods, where the rain was still dripping from the leaves. Twice, they came to a crossroads, but each time, the crumbs led them clearly down one of the paths. At the third crossroads, though, the trail of crumbs ended suddenly. "Maybe he ran out," Joe said.

"Or maybe they caught him at it," Frank said ominously. At the crossroads was a sign. Arrows pointed in opposite directions. One read, "Cathedral Forest Trail," and the other read, "Ice House."

"Ice House." Joe said. "What's that?"

"We saw it on the map, remember? It's from the old days, before refrigeration. People used to cut blocks of ice out of frozen ponds and keep them in buildings called ice houses."

"Well, which way do we go?" Joe asked.

"Nora and her group are searching around Cathedral Forest and the cliffs," Frank told him.

"To the Ice House, then," Joe said.

The two hustled down the path, which soon led to a large pond. Overlooking the pond was an old wooden building that resembled a broken-down barn. An iron crane with pincers on the end hung out from an opening on the second story. "That must be what they used to cut out and pick up the ice," Joe said.

The boys inched forward until they were just outside the building, and crouched under a broken windowpane in a side door of the Ice House. Inside, they heard Sherm's familiar voice! He was talking to the men from Resorts Horizons Industries.

"I want the rest of my money *now*," Sherm was saying. "Those boys are on to you, and before you know it, they'll be on to me."

"Now wait a minute, Sherm," Glenn answered. "Don't blame us if they're making trouble."

"Is it my fault that they've got nine lives?" Sherm retorted angrily. "I cut their rope when they were going over the cliffs, and they survived. I sawed the beams of the old Webster Shack so the roof would collapse on them, and they walked out with just a few bumps and bruises. For Pete's sake, I even shot an arrow at one of them!"

"You should have finished off the older one when you had him chloroformed," Bob's voice shot back. "That was the perfect chance to——"

"Look, guys," Glenn broke in. "Let's stay the course here. The plan is working. People are leaving the island, and a lot of houses are for sale. Once we relieve Dexter Greenleaf of the money he's been saving for taxes, and once we scare George Hubert out of the picture, Sherm will be able to dissolve the land agreement. That will give the corporation free rein on Makatunk. Any locals who remain at that point will be nothing but 'local color' at RHI's latest, greatest super-resort. And you, Sherm, can have your choice of a job as head of security, or a comfortable retirement in some warm, sunny place down south."

Just hearing them talk that way made Frank's blood boil. He was sure from the way Joe was clenching his fists that his brother felt the same way.

"Well, I still want my money now," Sherm insisted. "I've earned it by all I've done so far."

"Sherm," Glenn said calmly, "if you're so worried about the Hardy brothers, don't complain to us. Go get rid of them!"

"These guys make me sick," Joe muttered, straightening up. "I'm going in there."

It was an impulsive move, but Frank was behind him all the way. If these three turkeys thought they could destroy people's lives and take over Makatunk without a fight, they were dead wrong, he thought.

Frank prepared himself for action as Joe gave the door a swift karate kick. But as it flew open, accompanied by the sound of glass shattering, Frank froze in horror.

In front of them was Chet, gagged and bound to the giant iron chain of the antique pulley that drove the crane! His terrified eyes darted to the ceiling, twenty feet overhead to the rugged metal spikes of the huge gears that ran the pulley.

"This machine may look old and crude, but it still works on a very efficient pulley system," Bob said, snarling, picking up a hunting rifle and aiming it in the Hardys' direction. "So efficient, in fact, that it can mangle a person in just seconds. By way of warning, let me give you a little demonstration."

With that, Bob handed the rifle to Glenn, and walked to the nearby control levers, gripping them firmly in his hands. "Better say goodbye to your friend, boys."

16 In the Nick of Time

Frank and Joe were frozen by the large rifle that Glenn Carter now pointed their way. Through his gag, Chet let out a muffled scream of terror as Bob pulled the levers that set the heavy antique apparatus into motion. The huge iron links of the chain inched upward with a sickening screech, pulling Chet with them as they moved ever closer to the sharp teeth of the gears.

"What you're doing is cold-blooded murder!" Joe protested.

Bob shot him a sickly smile. "How convenient for us that the sheriff is right here," he said. "I'm sure his report on your friend's accidental death will be deemed believable. Especially since you boys won't be around to protest. You'll be at the bottom of the

141

ice pond, with heavy rocks tied to your ankles. No one will ever find you."

Chet's bound legs dangled frantically as he moved higher, held fast to the chain by ropes around his hands and waist.

Suddenly, Joe had an idea. "Good work, Chet!" he shouted loudly.

The diversion worked. In an instant, the surprised gunman's head turned toward Chet, just long enough for Joe to rush forward and grab the end of the rifle. Glenn yanked back on the weapon, and a loud blast rang out, smashing a hole in the ceiling of the old building.

At that instant, Frank tackled Bob and, reaching out with his right leg at the same time, kicked Sherm off balance for a crucial moment.

The gunshot had jolted Glenn, and with one sharp jab of his elbow to Glenn's solar plexus, Joe was able to wrest the weapon from his hands. Sherm had recovered enough to lunge for it, too, but a swift kick by Frank to the sheriff's midsection stopped him, doubling him over. Without turning, Frank then sent his elbow back into Bob's approaching head, catching him right on the nose.

Yowling with pain, Bob heaved a tight fist toward Frank's face. Bob had been blinded by the blow to his nose, though, and the punch was wild. Frank rammed his head into Bob's belly, and Bob fell backward, knocking his skull against the mechanism in the process. Bob collapsed on the floor, unconscious.

142

"Hmphlmgmph!" Chet tried to scream through the gag on his mouth. Looking up, Frank saw that his friend was only a couple of feet away from a grisly death, and still the mechanism ground on.

Joe finally got control of the rifle, but at that moment, Sherm, who had recovered, took a flying leap at Joe, sending him crashing to the floor. Again the gun went off. This time, a sharp pinging sound rang out from one of the gears suspended from the ceiling. The gun spun across the cement floor, sliding far to the other side of the large dark space. Joe tried to see where it was, but before he could spot it, both Glenn and Sherm were on him at once.

Joe's fists were flying, hitting Glenn again and again, first in the face, then with blows to the body. But now Frank saw that Sherm had grabbed a two-by-four and was about to smash it down on Joe's skull. Quickly, he leapt at the sheriff, landing a swift karate kick on his forearm. Yowling with pain, Sherm dropped the two-by-four and grabbed his broken wrist. In an instant, Frank was on him, finishing him off with a chop to the base of the skull. Frank turned around to help Joe, but help was no longer necessary. Joe stood panting over the crumpled form of Glenn Carter.

"The mechanism!" Frank shouted, glancing up at Chet, who was only inches from the teeth of the gears.

Joe leapt at the lever and grabbed it, yanking it down with all his strength. Frank ran to help him, and together the two brothers brought the mechanism to a screeching halt in the nick of time.

"Whew!" Joe said, stumbling backward, still out of breath. "That was close!"

"I wonder if this thing works in reverse," Frank said.

"Don't even try it!" Joe insisted. Climbing the links of the chain one by one, his Swiss Army knife between his teeth, he soon reached Chet and cut the ropes that bound him. The two of them climbed back down, as Frank checked on the men they'd knocked out. Glenn and Bob were still out cold. Sherm, while still conscious, lay crumpled in a corner, trying to catch his breath from the blows he'd taken. Frank reached down to the sheriff's waist and removed the set of handcuffs from his belt. "Thanks, Sherm," Frank said, cuffing Sherm's hands together. "It's great to have the law on your side when you need it."

Moments later, Joe and Chet joined him. Chet was wincing and rubbing his sore wrists. "My whole life flashed in front of my eyes when I was dangling on that thing, I swear it did!" Chet was still shaking from the terror of his experience. "I thought I was a dead man, for sure!"

"Well, Chet, I guess you've hung around with us long enough to know you've got another eight lives to go," Joe told him with a grin.

"This is where the gunshots must have come from!" came a sharp female voice from outside.

Frank looked over and saw Nora and the Acorn Society members staring at them from the doorway. "What's going on in here?"

"Well, for starters, we found Chet," Joe answered. "And while we were at it," he added, gesturing to the three men on the floor, "we solved the mystery of Makatunk Island."

Once the criminals were brought to town, all the islanders came together and worked quickly. Mr. Hubert and Nora Stricter made citizens' arrests of Sherm Davis and the men from RHI. They handcuffed them to a chain on the dock. When the weather cleared they would contact the mainland police to come take them away. A group of islanders and guests took turns watching the three, making sure they didn't try escaping during the two-hour wait.

"Dinner at the inn is on me tonight," Mr. Hubert announced loudly to the crowd, after the police boat had left with the criminals aboard. "And everyone on Makatunk is welcome. Vegetarian food only, of course," he said with a chuckle and a wink at Nora Stricter.

She smiled back at him and nodded appreciatively. "You're learning, Mr. Hubert. You're learning."

"I could use a shower," Joe said to Frank, wiping the sweat from his brow.

"Me, too," Frank agreed. "Maybe even a hot bath."

"I'm starving," Chet complained. "I didn't have any lunch. And I wasted a pocketful of perfectly good cookies, too."

The Hardys laughed and the three boys headed up the hill to Emma's house. As they climbed Hawk's Hill Road, the sun reappeared on the western horizon, below the dark bank of retreating clouds. It cast a bright rainbow on the eastern sky, indicating that the storm was over, and the island and its beauty were safe once more.

Later, the three friends returned to town, showered, refreshed, and ready for a good meal and a good party. Word must have spread about Mr. Hubert's dinner offer, because nearly everyone was there. Gabby greeted Frank, Joe, and Chet in turn with a clap on the back as they entered the dining room. As they stood in the doorway, the roomful of islanders burst into applause. The three boys flushed at all the attention.

"I'd like to give you an Acorn Society award for helping to keep Makatunk Island free and wild forever," Nora told the Hardys and Chet, stepping forward. She presented them with a pair of small acorns carved from wood. "Don't worry," she added. "The wood was not taken from a living tree. I keep a supply of dead wood to reward people who deserve it."

A murmur in the dining room caught Frank's attention, and he turned to the door. There stood Kent Halliwell, with her snowy hair piled up on her head and dark lipstick accenting her lips. In her hands was a small painting.

"I'm not staying for dinner," she said, walking into the room. "But when Dexter came by and told me about what happened, I wanted to come and bring you this."

She walked over to Frank, Joe, and Chet and handed them a matted watercolor of Cathedral Forest. The soft colors created a sense of the power and beauty of the place at dawn. Frank thought it was an extraordinary work of art.

"Wow, thanks," Joe said, admiring the piece, as people gathered around them and applauded.

Mr. Hubert stepped forward. "While we're all giving you our thanks," he said to Frank and Joe, "I'd like to add mine. Consider this inn your home away from home. Whenever you'd like a little peace and quiet, think of us up here on Makatunk—in spite of your experience this time!"

Everyone laughed at Mr. Hubert's joke, but they stopped when Dexter stepped forward, a sour look on his face.

"I'd like to say something, too," he said grimly. Frank noticed that he was wearing a clean, pressed white shirt. He had never seen the handyman in anything but work clothes and wondered what the occasion was.

"I'm not much for giving speeches," Dexter grumbled, "but these two boys helped us islanders out by getting rid of Sherm Davis. I've decided to do my bit to thank them. So, when I take their luggage down to the boat, I'm not gonna charge them one thin dime!" A sudden smile broke out on the big man's face, and reaching for Joe's hand, he pumped it up and down so hard that Joe winced in pain, even though he couldn't help laughing.

"Thanks, Dexter," Frank said, getting his own hand wrung now. "That's mighty big of you."

"Aw, it's nothing," Dexter said. "And if you ever come up again, I'll haul it free up the hill, too!"

"By the way," Mr. Hubert said, "we've all decided to put Makatunk's wild land in the hands of the State Conservancy Trust. That means it will be protected for all time from the kind of people who'd like to destroy it!"

A rousing cheer went up from the people in the dining room when they heard this news. No one clapped harder than Chet. "Well," Joe said, looking around at all the smiling faces gathered in the inn's dining room. "There's one thing they'll never ruin about Makatunk and that's the friendliness of its people."

"They sure came close," Gabby said, coming to the front of the crowd. "And they might have succeeded, too—if it weren't for the Hardy boys!"

NANCY DREW® MYSTERY STORIES By Carolyn Keene

LOOK FOR AN
EXCITING NEW
NANCY DREW MYSTERY
COMING FROM
MINSTREL® BOOKS
EVERY OTHER
MONTH

THE HARDY BOYS® SERIES By Franklin W. Dixon